ON THE TRAIN

The Urbana Free Library

To renew: call 217-367-4057
or go to *"urbanafreelibrary.org"*
and select "Renew/Request Items"

	DATE DUE	2~~13~~
~~MAR 3 0 2013~~		

BOOKS IN THE STELLAR GUILD SERIES

Tau Ceti by Kevin J. Anderson & Steven Savile
Reboots by Mercedes Lackey & Cody Martin

FORTHCOMING TITLES BY:

Robert Silverberg
Larry Niven
Eric Flint
Mike Resnick

ON THE TRAIN

HARRY TURTLEDOVE

SEQUEL NOVELLA BY
RACHEL TURTLEDOVE

THE STELLAR GUILD SERIES
TEAM-UPS WITH BESTSELLING AUTHORS

MIKE RESNICK
SERIES EDITOR

an imprint of

Rockville, Maryland

2—1
13°

Series edited by Mike Resnick.

ISBN: 978-1-61242-076-9

www.PhoenixPick.com
Great Science Fiction & Fantasy
Free Ebook every month

Published by Phoenix Pick
an imprint of Arc Manor
P. O. Box 10339
Rockville, MD 20849-0339
www.ArcManor.com

CONTENTS

A GREETING FROM THE SERIES EDITOR

GREETINGS, AND WELCOME TO ANOTHER *Stellar Guild* book.

The first two in the series have sold well enough that we can safely predict that the Stellar Guild will be around for a while, and that can only bode well for the future of science fiction. Because the purpose of the Stellar Guild is to team a superstar science fiction writer up with a protégé of his own choosing. The star writes a novella, the protégé writes a long novelette set in the same universe and shares a book that's guaranteed to get him or her better exposure than 98% of first novels do.

This particular team-up is a little more unique than most, because bestseller and Hugo winner Harry Turtledove chose to team up with his own very talented daughter. (Two generations of writers are not unheard-of in this field. My own daughter, Laura, won the 1993 Campbell Award for Best New Writer; Fritz Leiber's son Justin wrote some fantasy novels; Todd McCaffrey has taken over the Pern series after collaborating on a number of books with Anne before her death; and there have been a few others — but it's still a rarity.)

However, we're not publishing this because it's a rarity, but because we're convinced that it's a damned good book, and we think you'll agree long before you're halfway through it.

And keep your eye out for more Stellar Guild team-ups. We've got Robert Silverberg, Larry Niven, Eric Flint and their protégés under contract; Kevin J. Anderson and Mercedes Lackey and theirs are already in print; and we're negotiating with still more superstars who want to give their protégés a very visible platform from which to shine.

Mike Resnick

ON THE TRAIN

Book One
ALL ABOARD!

HARRY TURTLEDOVE

THE SUN BEAT DOWN on Pingaspor. Not much happened in the tropical town. What did happen mostly happened in slow motion.

Except when The Train pulled in.

A wise man somewhere along The Railroad once said, "You cannot step into The same Train twice." A wag somewhere else along The Railroad soon answered, "You cannot step into The same Train once." Yes, he was a wag, but maybe he wasn't so far wrong just the same. And passengers on The Train carried his words along with the wise man's to stops all along The Railroad: which is to say, to stops all around the world.

Javan had heard both sayings. He knew the truth of one of them, for he'd seen it with his own eyes. Sometimes The Train pulled into Pingaspor with smoke belching from a tall stack. Sometimes it glided into town almost as clean and silent as a dream. Once, not long before he was born, a team of elephants had brought The Train to the Pingaspor depot. Graybeards still chattered about that, in smokeshops and coffeehouses.

Once, before his great-grandfather was born, a team of dragons had pulled The Train into Pingaspor. These were not magic lands, so that created a great sensation. There were photographs of the day even yet, showing the dragons' huge red wings furled against their green, scaly hides. Of course everyone knew photographs lied, and could be made to lie in many different ways. If only someone had made a sketch! You could trust a sketch. At least half the Pingasporeans disbelieved the old story, photographs or no.

Javan himself did, at least half the time.

Up till now, he'd never had much to do with The Train. Oh, like any young man along The Railroad, he'd done his spell keeping the line in good repair. He'd shoveled dirt to shore up embankments. He'd spread gravel in the roadway. He'd swung a sledge, spiking new sleepers to the tracks to take the place of ties rotted through or eaten out by insect pests. Like any young man with an ounce of sense along The Railroad, he'd worked no harder than the overseers made him. It was something he had to do, not something he wanted to do. And the little bits of silver wire his labors won him did not inspire him to outdo himself. Oh, no—on the contrary.

But now mirrors of polished bronze were flashing from the west. The Train was on the way!

Because so little happened in Pingaspor, when something did word of it exploded through town like a shower of fire-works. Along with his kinsfolk and friends and neighbors, Javan hurried to the depot. Most of them wore no more than a strip of cloth to cover their loins. Some of the women covered their breasts with a similar strip, some supported them with one, and some did not bother doing either. Pingaspor lay on the equator; comfort was where you found it.

Javan, now, Javan wore a baggy cotton shirt, brightly dyed in stripes, and loose-fitting cotton trousers (not dyed at all). Sandals flipped and flopped on his feet. He clutched the leather handles of a carpetbag in his right fist. Unlike his friends and relations, he was dressed for a journey.

"You lucky polecat!" one of his friends said. Laughing, several others nodded.

"Am I, Uharto?" Javan said. "I don't know."

"Will you miss me?" asked a girl not far from his own age.

"Of course I will, Kiri," he answered, and she smiled at him. Her bare, pert breasts seemed to smile at him, too. Try-ing not to stare—it wasn't exactly rude, but it wasn't polite, either—Javan went on, "I expect I'll miss everything about Pingaspor. They don't do things our way all the time on The Train, or people say they don't."

Kiri pouted. That wasn't what she wanted to hear. Javan realized as much a few heartbeats too late. She wanted him to talk about her.

"I'll come back one day," he tried.

She tossed her head. Her hair flew in a blue-black cloud. "You'll be old by then, chances are," she said. "I expect I'll have found somebody else. I don't suppose I'll even remember your name. Patan, Jaman—what did we used to call that silly fellow?"

"I bet you'll remember me if I'm rich," Javan said.

"Well, maybe," Kiri admitted. People *did* get off The Train with fortunes: not very often, but they did. She tossed her head again. "If you're rich, I bet you won't remember me."

"Don't count coconuts till you've got them down from the tree," Uharto said. "C'mon." Along with the others, he swept Javan toward the ticket counter.

The man in the shade on the other side of the barred window couldn't have looked more bored if he were dead. "Your fare," he said, and held out his hand.

Javan had to remind himself that his pouch was in a pocket on the unfamiliar trousers. He opened it and shoved silver wire, and even a scrap of gold—a gift from an uncle who'd done well for himself—at the impassive clerk.

The man weighed the precious metal. "It will do," he said grudgingly. "Here is your ticket." It was printed in tiny type in several languages and folded over onto itself at least half a dozen times. In a sour voice, the man added, "You can take your place with the rest of the fools."

"He's jealous 'cause you're going and he's not," chubby Uharto said, his double chin wobbling as he spoke.

That jolted the clerk out of boredom. He threw back his head and laughed raucously. "Am I stupid enough to believe one place is better than another? I don't think so!"

Ticket in hand, Javan went out on the platform with kinsfolk and friends and neighbors. Only ticket-holders could go right to the edge; guards and ropes held back the rest. His friends slapped him on the back and pumped his hands.

Sniffling, his mother kissed him good-bye. Then Kiri did, too. He remembered that kiss a lot longer. When at last she broke away, he was amazed to find that her outline wasn't printed on the fabric of his shirt.

Only a couple of other passengers waited with him. One was a man of about forty—*an old man*, Javan thought—who held a carpetbag like his. The other was a woman of indeterminate age. She had a duffel, bigger than either man's bag, at her feet. Like him, they both wore more clothes than was common in Pingaspor. The man wiped his forehead with the back of his arm.

Javan peered down the long, straight track at the parallel rails that nevertheless seemed to meet somewhere before infinity. He smiled when he saw the first puff of smoke in the distance. "It's coming!" he exclaimed.

Both the older passengers leaned out to look, too. And they also both smiled. It wouldn't be long now! Soon The Train sounded its whistle: two long, sonorous blasts of steam to let Pingaspor know it was almost here. As if Pingaspor didn't already know!

As it slowed down to pull in to the depot, the older man said, "Now that's what The Train is supposed to look like." He spoke in tones of satisfaction, as if he would have been disappointed had it looked any other way.

Was there one Train or many? Towns all along The Railroad—towns all around the world—asked themselves the same question. Javan thought there was only one, but he wasn't sure. No one was sure, all around the world. Like so many large questions, that one might have been better argued than answered, anyhow.

Brakes squealing, locomotive chuffing, The Train eased to a stop. As the older man had said, this was the way The Train looked when you imagined it inside your head. The engine was a long, sleek 4-6-2, with drive wheels as tall as a man. The passenger carriages were of teak and mahogany and other expensive lumber, with fancy brasswork and a rococo flourishing of carvings and ornaments and gold leaf. What didn't gleam with bright metal gleamed with polished wood instead.

Even the freight cars were, well, clean. Some of them had writing on the sides, mostly in scripts that were only squiggles to Javan. Doors squealed open. Handlers in the blue livery of The Railroad handed boxes and crates and bales to the Pingasporean stevedores waiting to receive them. The local men and women gave back other bales and crates and boxes. Eventually, those would come off somewhere else. The boss handler took notes on a sheet of paper in a clipboard. The boss stevedore on the platform talked to a device he held in the palm of his hand. At other stops along The Railroad, it might work the opposite way.

Then Javan stopped worrying about anything so trivial as freight. The doors to three or four passenger carriages came open. In smooth unison, conductors set down wooden steps that led from the carriages to the platform. The conductors wore blue, too, blue of finer fabric and cut than the freight-handlers'. They had brimmed pillbox caps on their heads. There was a name for those....Kepis! Javan beamed when he came up with it.

In smooth unison, the conductors chorused, "Pingaspor! All out for Pingaspor!" That was in the local language, oddly accented. They said what was probably the same thing in other tongues, too. Javan recognized the name of his home city, but no more.

Only a handful of people got out. A tall woman's red hair made Javan gape—you heard about that kind of thing, but you hardly ever saw it here. A man with a hooked nose and fierce eyes wrapped himself in robes against the heat. A lizardy thing perched on his shoulder, as a tame bird might. It had fierce eyes, too, and sharp teeth. People out beyond the ropes squealed and waved at another man, a Pingasporean. He waved, too, but he looked unsure of himself. How long had he been away, if he didn't understand this was home?

Then Javan forgot him, too, for the conductors gave the call he'd been waiting to hear: "All aboard, Pingaspor! All aboard!"

He went up to the blue-uniformed man who stood closest to him and proudly displayed the ticket he and his family had scrimped and saved for so long to buy. If it impressed the fellow in the kepi, he hid it very well. He unfolded the ticket with unconscious skill, skimmed the fine print, and pulled out a paper punch, which he plied with might and main.

"You are in a third-class carriage. You understand? Third-class," he said, speaking slowly and carefully. No, Pingasporean wasn't his birthspeech. "You are in carriage number forty-three, bench five, place four. You understand? You read numbers?"

"Yes, I understand you. Yes, I can read numbers," Javan answered impatiently. He could read anything he pleased— well, anything in Pingasporean.

The conductor only shrugged. "All good, then. Welcome aboard." He waved Javan up the steps down which the red-haired woman had come a moment before.

Up Javan went, at a bound. The carriage in which he found himself was cooler than the platform had been; he suddenly found himself glad to be wearing more clothes than usual.

This was carriage number eleven: so it proclaimed in several languages and numbering systems. It was a second-class carriage, with padded seats that could recline. People—all kinds of people, wearing all kinds of clothes—stared at Javan. *Greenhorn!* He could read it in their eyes, no matter how exotic their features or coloring might have been.

Well, he was a greenhorn, but not so green that he couldn't figure out carriage forty-three would be farther from the engine than carriage eleven. Keeping his own eyes on the flowery carpet, he hurried down the aisle. He fumbled at the door; it used a latch he wasn't familiar with. But he made it work before anyone laughed out loud or, worse, got up to help him. And he did better when he opened the door into carriage twelve, and better still with the door that led out of it.

Third class, once he got to it, was a long step down from second. The seats were hard wooden benches. Some of the people sitting on them had cushions. Had they known to bring those along when they boarded? Javan wondered if he could make do with clothes from his carpetbag.

Bench five, place four. Sitting between him and his place was a woman old enough to be his mother. "Excuse me, but that's my seat," he said, pointing.

She replied in a clipped, economical tongue he'd never met before. He spread his hands to show he couldn't understand. She tried again, this time in the language of Kambok, the city just west of Pingaspor on The Railroad. Javan didn't speak it, but he knew it when he heard it. When she saw he still couldn't follow, she smiled, shrugged, moved her knees aside, and patted the empty space. That, he got. As he sat down, he saw that the wooden bench was also polished: not with spice-scented oils, but with the rubbing of backsides and spines uncountable—certainly by him. He wriggled, trying to get as comfortable as he could.

There was his Pingaspor, on the other side of the window glass. There was his family, his mother crying on his father's shoulder. There was Kiri, with the smiling breasts. He could still feel them, printed warm against his chest. He could still jump up, open the door, and go back to what he'd always known. He could...

He sat where he was, alone in the jam-packed carriage.

Handlers' shouts and thumps and jolts transmitted along the length of The Train told him they were getting ready to set out. The engineer blew a long, echoing blast on his steam whistle. Javan wondered what kind of fool he'd made of himself by coming aboard. *I'll find out*, he thought miserably.

The Train began to roll. After the first little jerk as the couplings went tight, it didn't seem to be moving at all. Rather, Pingaspor seemed to be unrolling in the opposite direction outside the window.

Unroll it did, faster and faster. Pretty soon—much too soon—he was out in the suburbs and the fields. Then they unrolled, too, and rank jungle sprang up on either side of The Railroad. A flash of scarlet against the green was a bird on the wing.

Javan watched it through a blur of tears he fought not to let fall. He was on The Train, bound for...whatever he was bound for. Pingaspor, everything he'd known in Pingaspor, Kiri—that all lay behind him now.

A snack-seller came down the aisle. He carried a tray of roasted bite-sized bits of meat and pearl onions on bamboo skewers. When he called out his wares, he used what sounded like the economical language Javan's benchmate had tried on him. People who bought talked with him in the same tongue, though by their looks and clothes they'd boarded at widely different stops on The Railroad.

Javan noticed that without thinking about it much. He didn't buy from the snack-seller. He had food for a couple of days inside his carpetbag. And the less he spent, the further the silver and the little bit of gold still in his pouch would stretch.

The Train stopped once late that afternoon, at a town called Namila. Javan knew as much about Namila as he knew about Kambok. It was the next stop on The Railroad. He'd never been there before. He didn't know anyone who had. He didn't know anyone from Namila who'd settled in Pingaspor, either.

Buildings in Namila were more angular than buildings in Pingaspor. They used more stone here, and less wood. The people were a little browner than Pingasporeans. Men and women here wore shirts and gauzy trousers cut fuller than the ones Javan had on.

A conductor came through the third-class carriage while The Train loaded and unloaded in Namila. One of the passengers—a burly man with a long blond braid and a bushy, red-gold beard—asked him something. They went back and forth in what sounded like the same speech the snack-seller and the woman next to Javan had used.

Taking his courage in both hands, Javan asked the conductor, "What language is that?"

When the man smiled, he showed a mouthful of gold teeth. Javan wondered whether he'd been born like that or used them to carry his wealth around in a form that was hard to steal. "This is Traintalk, sonny," he answered in slow, careful Pingasporean. "You just got on, huh?"

"That's right." Javan nodded. "A few hours ago."

"Didn't think I recognized you. You keep your ears open, that's all. Traintalk's easy to pick up. It's got to be, so people from all over can learn it." He nodded once, gruffly, as if to remind himself he had more important things to do. Then he went and did them—or at least he went away.

Javan turned to the woman sitting beside him. "Traintalk?" he asked.

She smiled and nodded. Her nod was much friendlier than the conductor's. "*Sim*," she said, and nodded again. "*Sim*."

He realized *sim* had to mean *yes*. "*Sim*," he echoed, trying to say the vowel the same way she had. "Traintalk!"

He wanted to learn everything at once. He knew he couldn't, but he wanted to anyhow. He pestered the woman till she shook her head and spoke with finality: "*Bou*." That plainly meant *no*. She thought the lesson was over. Even if she did, she'd taught him another word.

A young woman from Namila walked through the third-class carriage. She didn't stop, but went on to one farther back. Instead of using a carpetbag or a duffel, she carried her things in a pack she strapped over her shoulders.

Javan's eyes followed her. She wasn't as pretty as Kiri—nowhere near. But Kiri had vanished behind him along with the rest of Pingaspor. The Namilan woman wasn't homely, either. She gave Javan something to think about for a little while.

The Train began to roll with that jerk he'd felt before. He took a bookreader out of his carpetbag. He had trouble paying attention to the story he'd picked, though. He kept peering out the window and getting distracted.

Rain drummed down on the carriage's roof. It got dark outside. A couple of people stood up as the lights in the carriage came on. One of them patted his belly, so Javan supposed they were on their way to a dining car. A different snack-seller came through. This fellow was selling spicy fish and grilled vegetables wrapped in flatbread. He did a brisk business.

Those savory smells made Javan's stomach growl. He dug into the carpetbag again. He spooned up noodles and smoked shrimp and nagwa beans: the tastes of home. Idly, he wondered whether the young woman from Namila had brought food along, and what they ate there.

By the time he finished his supper, night had fully fallen. He tried the bookreader again, but it couldn't hold his interest. He shifted on the hard bench. How was he supposed to sleep?

With pantomime, he tried asking his seatmate. He learned how to say *sleep* in Traintalk, but her answer seemed to be *You've got to figure it out for yourself.*

She had a pillow that hissed itself full of air when she pressed a red spot on it. She still had to sleep sitting up, but it cradled her neck and the back of her head. Eyeing the pillow with sea-green jealousy, Javan realized he could have done a better job of readying himself for his journey.

He could have, but he hadn't. He had to make the best of what he had brought along. If he rolled up some clothes…

He passed a perfectly awful night. He wasn't used to sleeping sitting up. He wasn't used to sleeping in a carriage whose motion he could feel. And he really wasn't used to sleeping in a carriage full of talking, snoring, farting strangers. He would have sworn he never closed his eyes at all—but sunrise ahead of The Train caught him by surprise.

He yawned and stretched. He felt stiff as a corpse. His back crackled like a shaken sack of nutshells. And his mouth fell open when he looked out the window. All he saw was ocean.

He'd never seen—he'd never dreamt of—so much water all in one place before. Of course The Train girdled the world, so of course it crossed both land and sea. He knew as much—who didn't? But to know it and to experience it proved two very different things.

A flying fish flapped up alongside The Train. It paced Javan's carriage for a little while, staring in with an unwinking yellow gaze. Then it banked away and flew off in pursuit of food or love or whatever else its fishy heart desired.

How deep was the water under the tracks here? On what sort of pylons did The Railroad rest? Javan could ask himself the questions, but couldn't answer them. If magic ruled this part of the world, maybe it held up the tracks.

If The Train girdled the world, how did ships cross from the northern hemisphere to the southern and the other way around? That question Javan had answered for him before midday. He could not see how The Railroad climbed above the ocean, but he could see that it did. A three-masted sailing ship—it was a schooner, but Javan knew nothing of schooners—sailed toward The Railroad, heading north. He could tell that it would pass under the tracks with room to spare.

What happened when a storm blew up? If there were storms on land, weren't there bound to be storms at sea?

Down from its height came The Train. Land—not a lot of land—replaced water. The Train chuffed to a halt. "Liho! This stop is Liho!" conductors called in several languages. One of the tongues was Traintalk; Javan recognized it now. "You can get out and stretch your legs here, folks."

The little island of Liho belonged to The Railroad. The Train took on coal and water and supplies. Javan eyed the locomotive. It was stubbier than it had been in Pingaspor, with a taller smokestack. Maybe they'd changed engines at a stop during the night. Maybe, but Javan didn't think so. He was sure he would have noticed. Maybe the engine had just... changed.

People from The Train streamed toward the eatery built into the depot. *Fredarvi*, the sign above it said in characters Javan could read—and, presumably, in other writing systems as well. He wondered what it meant. Maybe it was a Traintalk word, one he hadn't learned yet.

The warm, damp breeze wafted savory smells his way. He fought temptation, fought and lost. He'd have to start eating things he hadn't brought from Pingaspor sooner or later. Why not sooner? He joined the stream going into the Fredarvi eatery.

A boy on the edge of manhood—a boy not too much younger than Javan, in other words—led him to a table and set a menu in front of him. A couple of minutes later, a serving woman bustled up and spoke to him in Traintalk. He spread his hands to show he couldn't follow. But the menu had pictures. He pointed at some things that looked good. She nodded and hurried away.

Faster than he'd expected, the food came. It tasted as good as it looked—he could think of no higher praise. He started to tear into it like a starving forest cat, afraid The Train would leave without him unless he hurried. Then he noticed the other passengers were going slower. They ate as if they knew they had time.

He paid for his lunch with silver wire. It was cheaper than he'd expected, too. And he learned how to say *thank you* in Traintalk.

A gong sounded. A voice spoke from the air, in one language after another: "The Train leaves in ten minutes. Take your seats, please. All aboard!" Javan understood the Pingasporean announcement. And he caught the words for *The Train* in Traintalk.

He sighed when he sat down on the shiny wooden bench in the third-class carriage. The chair in the Fredarvi eatery had been softer and better molded to his backside. But the eatery stayed here, on the little island of Liho in the middle of the sea. The Train—The Train was going places.

How big was this sea? Javan saw nothing but water from the time The Train left Liho till the sun set behind the caboose. He ate supper out of his carpetbag, and sighed again. When he remembered that delicious lunch, what he'd brought along seemed dull.

After a while, the woman beside him inflated her clever pillow and went to sleep. Javan went through another miserable night—maybe not quite so bad as his first, but anything but good. He had another fit of envy when he remembered the reclining seats in the second-class carriages. You could lean back and relax in one of those.

And that was only second class! What was first class like? He hadn't been in one of those carriages. He could imagine real beds in them. He could imagine smiling pretty girls climbing into those beds with men, and smiling handsome men climbing into them with women. That would make sure a passenger slept well, all right.

He could imagine anything he pleased—and he did, till at last he dozed off. Then a baby two rows behind him started to scream. He woke with a start. The mother sang a soft lullaby in Traintalk. The baby went on screaming. Javan wanted to bang his head against the window frame. If he knocked himself cold, he might get some rest. He didn't think he was likely to otherwise.

The lavatory car that served the third-class carriages had two shower stalls for men on one side of the aisle and two for women on the other. Many passengers stayed on The Train for a long time. They needed to get clean.

If you wanted, you could wash up in the middle of the night. You were less likely to have to wait then. Javan did that several times right after he boarded The Train. It wasn't as if he were sleeping much anyhow.

But, little by little, he started to get used to things. He was as proud of the first time he slept through the night as a mother is when her newborn does it in a cradle. If he slept during the night, though, he had to wash during the day with most of the other people.

More often than not, that meant he had to queue up and wait his turn. He didn't like standing in line, but what else could you do? People who were able to talk to one another passed the time that way. Javan soaked up Traintalk like a blotter. He started to be able to do some talking himself.

One day, he came out of a shower stall and started back to his carriage just as the young woman who'd boarded at Namila a few hours after he did was about to go into one. He nodded to her. "Hello," he said. "Day is good?"

"Day is good, *sim*, thank you." She nodded back. "Hello." She was as much a beginner as he was.

"Hello." He said it again, and then, plunging, "Name is to—uh, for—you?"

"Luisa. Name is Luisa," she said. "Name is for you?"

"Luisa." He repeated that, too. Then he jabbed a thumb at his own chest. "Name is Javan."

"Javan," she said gravely. "Hello, Javan." She stepped into her stall. The latch clicked behind her.

Javan squeezed up the aisle and back toward his carriage. Some of the older people waiting in line smiled at the byplay between him and Luisa. Some of them talked about it, too. Luckily for Javan, he couldn't follow what they were saying yet.

Luisa wasn't the only thing on his mind. He had to eat. He'd come aboard with some money, but not a lot. Food on The Train wasn't expensive, but it did cost something. If his silver wire left his pouch and nothing came in…That story had only one ending, and it wasn't happy.

People played cards and dice on The Train. It helped make time pass, and it redistributed the wealth. When some of Javan's scanty wealth got redistributed to the big man with the blond braid and the bushy beard, he decided he had to find a different way to keep going.

That evening, when one of the snack-sellers came through the carriage, Javan asked him, "You need helper?"

The man shook his head. "*Bou*." He paused, considering. "But maybe Siilo does. He's kind of old and creaky."

"Siilo. With the white goatee?" Javan used his fingers to show the few wispy hairs the man proudly let sprout from his chin.

Laughing, the snack-seller nodded. "*Sim*, that's Siilo. You ask. Maybe he'll say yes. Maybe he'll tell you to—" Javan didn't quite get what Siilo might tell him to do, which had to be just as well.

He waited a little while, hoping Siilo might bring his tray through the carriage. When the man with the straggly chin beard didn't, Javan went looking for him. He caught up with him two carriages farther back. "You need helper?" he asked brusquely—he still wasn't good enough in Traintalk to be anything but brusque.

Siilo looked him over. Then he pointed to the end of the carriage. "Go wait in vestibule. Let me finish working this carriage. Then we talk."

Javan understood just enough of that to do as he was told. The vestibule was tiny and gloomy. When Siilo joined Javan there, the snack-seller's tray kept prodding the younger man.

"You going to get off soon?" the snack-seller demanded in angry, suspicious tones. His tray prodded Javan again. This time, Javan was convinced Siilo poked him on purpose. Fiercely, Siilo went on, "You get off soon, I don't waste my time on you. I find somebody who stay around a while."

People did make short hauls on The Train. They went somewhere a quarter of the world away for business, or for schooling. Or they had family or friends scattered along The Railroad. Javan envied people like that. They knew where they were going, and why.

But he wasn't a person like that. The world ahead, the time ahead, remained a continual surprise for him. All he wanted to see was what happened next. "Not get off soon," he said in his still-fragmentary Traintalk. "I ride."

"You sure?" Siilo plainly did his best to look into Javan's head and read what was printed on the folds of his brain. "You tell me lies, I break you in half, you hear? I not so young, but I plenty strong. Mean, too." He inflated his scrawny chest.

Though Javan wasn't a big man (few Pingasporeans were), the top of Siilo's head didn't come up to his eyes. The snack-seller had to be three times his age. Somehow, though, the thought of an angry Siilo didn't make him laugh the way it should have.

"Sure," Javan said. "*Sim*, I sure."

"All right." Siilo sounded as if he hoped it was. "Next question is, you work or you just screw around?"

"I work." Javan did his best to sound positive. He threw back a question of his own: "You pay?"

"Not much," Siilo answered bluntly. "Food—enough to keep you going, not enough to make you fat. You steal from me, you never work for nobody on The Train, not never again. You hear? You follow?"

"I hear. I follow." The thought of stealing had crossed Javan's mind. So had the thought that Siilo would be watching him. If you ran out of money on The Train, and if you couldn't get any by working, what would you do? What *could* you do? Sooner or later—probably sooner—you'd have to get off. And if having to get off The Train wasn't the worst defeat in the world, Javan couldn't imagine what would be.

"All right." Again, Siilo didn't seem sure it was. "You work good, maybe—maybe, I say—you get a little money, too. A bargain?"

"A bargain," Javan said, wondering what he was getting into.

"Good." Siilo held out his hand. Javan clasped it. The snack-seller's grip was firm. He might be skinny, but he was no weakling. After the handshake, he asked, "You cook?"

"Little bit." Javan held his thumb and forefinger close together.

Siilo laughed again. "You will eat your own cooking, that what you do. You get better plenty fast then. I show you what I know. Not hard. But you got to pay attention. You make stuff so bad I can't sell it, you don't eat at all that day."

"You cook, maybe? I carry tray?" Javan asked.

"*Bou*." Siilo dismissed the notion with a wave. "Your Traintalk not good enough yet. You learn some more, then maybe we see. Eh?"

"*Sim.*" Javan sighed out the agreement. He had to hope he wouldn't pass too many days with an empty belly.

Siilo bought meat and produce from the cooks who fixed fancier meals for the dining cars. When he brought Javan along to show him how they haggled, the cooks made a great show of being friendly. They put their well-fed arms around Javan's shoulder. They popped snacks into his mouth.

Siilo laughed that old man's cynical laugh again. "You never trust these bastards. They screw you good if you give 'em the chance. Now they just try to soften you up."

"Oh, what a sour fool you are, Siilo!" one cook said.

"What a liar, too!" another added. The more they protested, the more Javan believed Siilo.

The snack-sellers couldn't use the cooks' fancy kitchens. Instead, they were crowded together in a converted—a barely converted—freight car. Each one had his or her grill and tiny counter. Iceboxes kept food fresh. Chains and stout locks on the iceboxes kept food safe.

Siilo showed Javan how to adjust the blue flame that heated the grill. It seemed simple enough. Javan was rash enough to say so. "Simple enough now, yes," Siilo answered; the man with the white, wispy beard seemed to hold on to his patience with both hands. "But you got to cook with coal, with wood, with whatever we can get. Sometimes..." His voice trailed away.

Javan remembered the stories about the time elephants had pulled The Train into Pingaspor. He remembered the old, old photographs of the dragons. Did Siilo expect him to sizzle meat and fry tubers over the flame that came from, say, a very small dragon? He couldn't even ask the question. He didn't have the words for it, not in Traintalk.

Above the grill was a small cabinet, also under lock and key. Siilo stashed his spices there. Two shakes from this jar, one from that, a pinch from a third just before things were done... "These others, they all have their own ways to make things," Siilo said. "Some pretty good, but what I teach you, that's the best."

One of the other snack-sellers jeered at him: "You can say it, but that doesn't make it so."

"Are you talking or farting, Darvish?" Siilo retorted. Everyone laughed but Darvish, who was the butt of the joke, and Javan, who didn't get it.

He was busy all the time. He went back to his hard seat only to sleep. He was so tired when he did that it stopped bothering him. What did bother him was that he hardly saw Luisa any more. When at last he did run into her, it was in the queue for the shower stalls again.

"Where have you been?" she asked him. Her Traintalk was getting better, as was his.

"Working." Javan mimed chopping and flipping pieces of meat. Then he peeled imaginary tubers and chucked the skins into an equally imaginary rubbish bin.

"Oh," she said. "Good for you. Pretty soon I have to find something to do, too." She made a face. "That or get off."

"It's a good ride." Javan's mouth twisted in a smile more like Siilo's than he knew. "Or I think so. Now that I work, I don't get to see out much."

"No, I guess not." Luisa took a couple of steps toward the stalls. So did Javan. She went on, "I thought you were staying away from me on purpose."

"Why would I do that?" Javan asked in surprise.

"I don't know. But I thought you had some reason, or else you had another friend." Luisa slid into one of the stalls on the women's side. The water in there began to run. She couldn't have heard what Javan answered even had he known what to say.

When Siilo used a blue flame, gas from a tank fed that flame through a complicated system of tubes and valves. One morning, Javan had trouble coaxing the flame alight. He checked to make sure the burner outlet was clean so the gas could slide out and burn. Everything seemed fine, but he still had trouble lighting it.

He looked around the crowded converted freight car. Some of the other snack-sellers and assistants were struggling with their grills, too. Others were doing things that didn't need fire, like kneading dough and chopping vegetables. And a couple just stood around not doing anything, which was something you hardly ever saw in that busy place.

"What's going on?" Javan asked after trying once more to light the grill and not having any luck.

One of the men standing around answered him: "We're right on the edge of Dongorland, that's what." Bordric wasn't quite as old as Siilo, but he sure wasn't young. He was of the same race as the big man with the blond braid in Javan's carriage. He was tall and fair like that fellow, but bald on top. His beard had probably been fiery once; now it was mostly gray.

"And so?" Javan wasn't sure he'd even heard of Dongorland. Pingaspor didn't have much to do with it.

"And so wait a little while," Bordric said.

Javan clicked his tongue between his teeth: an unhappy noise. If he stood there waiting for he didn't know what and Siilo came in and caught him...That wasn't a pretty picture. He tried to busy himself with vegetables. Every so often, he'd fiddle with the grill, but he couldn't make it catch.

Siilo did come in. Javan waited for his boss to clout him over the head with his tray. But Siilo took in what was happening at a glance. "Dongorland," he said, and muttered to himself in a language that wasn't Traintalk. "It's pretty, but...." He shook his head.

Pretty? That hadn't even occurred to Javan. Since he'd started working for Siilo, he'd been too busy for anything more than occasional glimpses of the outside world. One of the reasons he'd got on The Train to begin with was to see more of what lay along The Railroad than Pingaspor alone. And he had, but not so much more as he'd expected when he came aboard.

Bordric bent over and peered down through the bars of his grill into its guts. When he straightened, he let out a grunt. "All right," he said. "I think we're in business again."

"About time," another snack-seller said. He put meat on his grill. The sizzle announced that it was working.

Puzzled, Javan looked between the bars of Siilo's grill. The gas nozzle wasn't down there. Neither was the baby dragon he'd imagined. But a small salamander smiled up at him. The little magical creature took the nozzle's place. It glowed yellowish red. The heat coming off it scorched the tip of Javan's nose and dried out his eyeballs. He pulled back from the grill in a hurry.

"Oh," he said. Here was more proof the world was bigger and more complicated than it looked to be in the place where he was born and raised. "Dongorland is this kind of place."

"Dongorland is this kind of place," Siilo agreed. "You tell the salamander how hot you want the grill, it make the grill that hot. But you got to treat it good. Don't just let it eat the drippings from the meat. Feed it scraps—feed it scraps from what you get yourself, not from what I sell. You keep it happy, it cook fine for you. Better than a blue flame, even. But you make it mad, look out! Either it go cold or it burn off your stupid eyebrows."

"Tell it how hot?" Javan floundered. "Does it understand Traintalk?" He eyed the salamander again, cautiously. It was still smiling, still glowing. He hoped that meant it was happy.

"It understand *you*," Siilo said. "Speak whatever speech you please. It feel what is in your heart, what is in your head."

"All right," Javan answered, anything but sure it was.

As the younger man and the older one talked, the quality of the light inside the converted freight car changed. Shadows that had been steady started to move. If you grew up in Pingaspor or places like Pingaspor, you were used to lamps that stayed in one place. In Dongorland, evidently, they were used to will-o'-the-wisps that swooped and flickered across the ceiling and the tops of the walls. The amount and color of the light they gave wasn't much different from what had come out of the lamps. The impression was.

"Do I have to keep them happy, too?" Javan asked.

"*Bou.*" Siilo laughed at the idea. "They always happy. Put your hand up to one."

Hesitantly, Javan did. He couldn't touch the will-o'-the-wisp. If you could touch one, he supposed, it wouldn't be a real will-o'-the-wisp. This one slipped through and past his fingers. As it did, he heard, or imagined he heard, the faintest laughter somewhere deep inside his mind.

"Take a look inside the ice chest." Siilo's voice was sly.

Javan did. The ice chest ran off a wire, the way the grill ran off its gas line. It had in Pingaspor and points west, anyhow. Not in Dongorland. When Javan unlocked it now, a little blue-green creature, all covered in rime, looked out at him. Its breath made his toes want to shiver in his sandals. That breath had to be the coldest thing he'd ever felt.

He knew, at least, the proper name for the salamander. For this? No. "What do you call it?" he asked as he closed the ice chest's door.

"Ice elemental," Siilo answered. "It like brandy—strong brandy, so the stuff don't freeze right away. Same as with the salamander, you got to keep it happy."

"Does it get drunk?" Javan asked.

"*Bou, bou.*" Siilo shook his head. "Brandy is like food for it."

"Food. Right." Javan waved his hands. Again, he almost but not quite touched a will-o'-the-wisp. Again, it laughed inside his mind. "How long are things like…this?"

"Till they aren't any more," Siilo said. "Now get cracking. No matter how things are, people got to eat. I got to sell them stuff."

But Javan, for once, didn't spring into action when the snack-seller told him to. "Maybe they eat fairy dust here," he said.

"Some of them do," Siilo answered with a matter-of-fact shrug. "But I don't sell it. They got to buy it in the dining car. You make nice to the salamander, grill me up some more meat

cubes for the skewers. What I do, I got to keep on doing."
Away he went.

Make nice to the salamander? Javan did his best. He fed
it shreds of meat. He told it how he wanted the grill. And
he sang it a song young men in Pingaspor sang when they
cheered on their battleball side.

He had no idea if that helped. He couldn't see how it
would hurt. Whether because of the song or in spite of it, the
salamander gave him just the heat he wanted. He sprinkled
on the spices the way Siilo had taught him. He hadn't been
cooking long enough to try ideas of his own.

When Siilo came back to fill his tray, he tasted what Javan
had done. After a judicious pause, he said, "Not bad."

"Thanks." Not just the salamander's heat warmed Javan—
Siilo didn't praise lightly. "Er—Siilo?"

"What you want?" the old man asked gruffly.

"What happens if I take the ice elemental out of the
chest and drop it on the salamander?" Javan illustrated with
gestures.

Siilo's eyebrows leaped. "You freeze your hands. Then you
get burned bad. Then you get in big trouble, if you still around
to get in trouble. That's what."

"But what happens to the ice elemental and the salamander?"

"You don't want to find out. Believe me, you don't." The
snack-seller loaded the tray and left in a hurry.

After he was gone, Bordric said, "He's right, kid—you
don't. A long time ago, even before Siilo got on The Train,
somebody did that. They buried the fool's frozen ashes in a
jam tin. A *little* jam tin. And they buried some other people
who didn't do anything but stand too close to him. *And* they
had to fit out a new car for folks like us. *And* The Train got
thrown off schedule."

The way he said that made it plain that being late was the
worst disaster. Fitting out a new car? Very sad—expensive,
too. Innocent people getting killed? Tragic. But The Train
couldn't be late.

Bordric eyed Javan, who realized he had to say something. He did: "All right. I won't do anything stupid. I just wondered, that's all."

"Well, now you know," Bordric growled. His knife flashed as he sliced red and yellow peppers. Javan went back to slicing, too, and didn't introduce the ice elemental to the salamander.

The Train pulled into the city of Dongor late that afternoon. Javan was back in the third-class carriage when it did. He'd wheedled a little time off from Siilo: "I've never seen a magic city before! Why ride The Train if I can't see magic once in a while?"

"Oh, go on." Siilo cuffed him on the side of the head—more affectionately than not, but not altogether. "Good thing for you you don't do this kind of silly stuff all the time, though, or I tell you no for sure."

Dongor looked like—well, a magic city. In the distance, on a hill, Javan saw a castle with a tall white tower reaching for the sky. Dragons flew through the air. So did smaller gryphons and hippogriffs. Smaller still were…what was the name for those? Were they wyverns? If they weren't, he didn't know what a wyvern would be.

A highway led north from the depot. In Pingaspor and other cities where sorcery didn't work, a highway would have been paved with stone, or perhaps with asphalt. Beasts or engines would have powered the wagons and carriages that traveled it.

Here, the highway shimmered like mother-of-pearl under the sun. A carpet piled high with crates glided along it, floating waist-high above that gleaming surface. Next to the carpet rode a man whose robe sparkled with silvery threads. His mount was not a tricycle or a horse but a unicorn.

And yet the people at the Dongor depot didn't seem much richer, if at all, than the people who thronged the streets of Pingaspor. Plenty of them were skinny, the way Javan had been skinny when he climbed aboard The Train. Ordinary people—people who weren't wizards directing flying carpets—didn't have clothes shot through with silver. Quite a few of them hardly had any clothes, silvery or not.

Magic, Javan realized, did about the same tricks the mechanical arts did in other parts of the world. It got people things they needed and made them more comfortable than they would have been without it. If it did those tricks a great deal better than the mechanical arts did, Javan couldn't prove that by what he saw at the depot. It was just…different.

Then again, some of the people waiting at the depot in Dongor were…different, too. A pair of wingety fairies—Javan could find no other name for them—boarded a first-class carriage.

When The Train left Dongor, it wasn't with the bellow of a steam whistle. These warning blasts came from the throats of living things. Were dragons hauling the carriages and freight cars? From his place inside one, Javan couldn't see. But what else could come out with an unearthly bellow like that?

As soon as The Train began to move, he hopped up and hurried back to Siilo's grill. The snack-seller would come out with an unearthly bellow of his own if he decided Javan was goofing off. He'd let Javan have a favor. Javan knew he wouldn't get another one any time soon if Siilo thought he was taking advantage of him.

When Siilo came back to fill up his tray, Javan said, "You go up to first class. Did you see the fairies?" The last word came out in Pingasporean. He mimed wings to show what he meant.

"Fairies." Siilo said it in Traintalk. "Yes, I go up there. They don't buy anything from me yet. Too bad. Fairies tip good when they buy."

"When we leave Dongorland—when we leave magic—do they keep their wings?" Javan asked. He gestured at the grill, and at the smiling salamander that kept it hot. One of these days, he supposed it would start burning gas again, or maybe chunks of hardwood.

"They keep wings, yes. But they don't fly without magic—wings aren't strong enough." Siilo plucked at his white goatee. "I don't *think* they fly without magic. I never see them do it."

"All right," Javan said. Siilo gave straight answers. Javan didn't always like his boss—liking someone who worked him so hard wasn't easy—but he did respect him.

A day and a half after leaving the city of Dongor, The Train stopped at a depot called Thargorond. Thargorond proved to be an island in the middle of a lake. Mountains rose in the distance. Like Liho, this was a place where The Train was serviced, and so, also like Liho, it was a place where passengers and crew could get out to stretch their legs.

Siilo didn't give Javan anything special to do while most people were getting off. The old man knew how much he could demand. He didn't ask for more than that...most of the time, anyhow.

When Javan jumped down onto the platform, he was pleased to see that the Thargorond depot boasted a Fredarvi eatery. He was even more pleased at the idea of eating food he hadn't cooked himself. And he was most pleased of all when Luisa said she'd go into the eatery with him.

She was serving meals in one of the dining cars now. That meant they both looked at the Fredarvi establishment through eyes different from the ones that had discovered the eatery on the oceanic island.

But they talked more about what they'd been doing themselves. "We have to figure out how to get together more," Javan said.

Luisa nodded. "*Sim*," she said; only afterwards did he realize how crushed he would have been had she answered *bou*.

Everything was the same at this Fredarvi establishment as it had been in the one at the Liho depot. And everything was different. The tables were made from different wood. Different fabrics covered the chairs, which were made in a different style. Will-o'-the-wisps took the place of LEDs or fluorescent tubes or whatever the other eatery had used for light. No doubt the cooks roasted and broiled and boiled with

salamanders rather than gas or coal. And no doubt ice elementals kept raw food cold and the air inside the eatery cool.

But that air *was* cool, as it had been at the Liho depot.
The furniture here was comfortable, as it had been there. The
servers here were also friendly and brisk. And the food was
good and quick and cheap.

Javan raced through his meal the way he had at Liho,
but for a different reason. Then, he'd feared The Train would
leave without him. He knew better now. But he did want to
see the handlers fueling it.

He hadn't cared about that at Liho, not to the extent of
a fingernail's length of lead wire he hadn't. So they put wood
or coal or rock oil or whatever they put into the tender behind
the locomotive. So what? Unless you ran on wood or coal or
rock oil yourself, why would you care?

When they fed the dragons, though...The photographs
he'd seen in Pingaspor both had and hadn't done the great
beasts justice. Those photographs hadn't been adobed all out
of recognition. These green-scaled, crimson-winged beasts
were plainly of the same kind as the ones that had amazed his
home city by bringing in The Train one day long vanished in
the great backward and abysm of time. The colors, the shapes,
the dimensions were about what he would have expected.

But no photographs, not even the most perfect thridi ones
that pretended to be realer than real, came close to conveying
the power and majesty inherent in dragonkind. Seen for real,
seen and heard and smelled (a mixture of old serpent and hot
metal), the presence dragons had was like a blow to the face.

And when you fueled dragons, you didn't give them wood
or coal or rock oil. Oh, no! The pair that were pulling The
Train through this stretch of Dongorland tore at the carcasses of some beasts that would have been great except in
comparison to them. The stink of blood warred with drag-
onmusk. Dragons' teeth were as long as swords, and as sharp,
but thicker. Would they even notice slicing up a man? The
ancient wisdom smoldering in the dragons' golden eyes ar-

gued that they would. Whether they would care was another question altogether.

Luisa's hand found Javan's. "They scare me," she said in a small voice.

"They scare me, too," Javan answered. He hadn't known a dragon's tongue was prickly like a cat's, and for the same reason: to rasp all the meat off the bones. On a dragon's tongue, though, the prickles were as long as his fingers. After a moment, Javan went on, "I bet they scare everybody—everybody with any sense, anyhow. But they're wonderful."

She didn't come right out and call him a liar. She also didn't look as if she believed him.

Passengers had been boarding The Train by ones and twos. When a warning gong sounded, they streamed out of the depot and away from the dragons, which by then had stripped almost all the flesh from the bones in front of them—and had crunched the bigger bones for marrow.

As Javan climbed up into his carriage, he asked a conductor, "Do the dragons ever eat their handlers by mistake?"

"Their handlers? *Bou!*" The pudgy man in the blue kepi sounded shocked. Then he laid a finger by the side of his nose and went on in a low voice: "Every once in a while, though, an especially obnoxious passenger disappears."

"Oh, really?" Javan said.

"Really," the conductor assured him. "I wouldn't tell you that if I didn't know Siilo's taken you under his wing. Siilo's all right, Siilo is."

"I think so," Javan answered.

"You'd better, kid. You'd better." The conductor's double chin wobbled softly as he nodded in agreement with himself. "Don't think you're the first sprout he's ever given a hand to. Yes, Siilo's all right."

"Quit your gabbing, you two, and let me by," a grouchy woman behind Javan said. Javan took his own place. The carriage was filling up fast now. Screams from the dragons warned that The Train was about to get rolling. They also woke the baby whose parents sat a couple of rows in back of

Javan. The baby's screams were tiny next to those from the dragons, but they were much closer and on a shriller, more annoying note. And they went on and on, which the dragons' screams didn't.

Obnoxious passengers, the conductor had said. Javan couldn't think of many more obnoxious than that loud-mouthed baby. Unlike adults, the baby probably couldn't help it. Javan understood as much. He still wondered if the brat might make a dragon a tasty snack, or if it was too small to notice.

Well, he didn't have to stay here and listen to it. He headed back to the converted freight car. He could listen to the chatter of the snack-sellers and their helpers instead. He could even join in if he felt like it—and if he found the time.

Before long, he got lost in his work, the way he did more often than not. Siilo didn't just take you under his wing. Once he got you there, he squeezed you and shaped you till you were the way he wanted you to be. He didn't realize he was doing it. For a long time, you might not realize he was doing it, either. Whether you realized it or not, it happened all the same.

As Javan had got used to cooking with the blue flame, so he got used to cooking with the salamander. It was friendlier than the blue flame had been—it was as long as he kept it happy, anyhow. In the parts of the world that worked by the mechanical arts, things were just things. Here in this magical land, things also had personalities. People born and raised in these lands had to take that for granted, and to find the mechanical arts strange and impersonal and intriguing. For Javan, it worked the other way around.

One morning, he got to Siilo's grill before the sun came up. He usually did—it wasn't as if he didn't have plenty to do. He looked down into the grill, ready to greet the salamander. He'd grown fond of it, and of the ice elemental. Now that he knew them, he couldn't imagine tormenting one with the other.

But the salamander wasn't there.

Javan swore—in Pingasporean. You could cuss up a storm in Traintalk. The snack-sellers were fluently, even poetically, profane in it. But Javan was still new to the language. He didn't get the satisfaction swearing in it that he did in his native tongue.

He also didn't get the grill started. The salamander wasn't there, but neither was the gas jet with which he'd cooked before. Javan stood in front of the grill scratching his head. He'd beaten everybody else into the converted freight car, so he had no one to ask what to do.

Siilo wouldn't be happy if he came in to fill up his tray and found the grill cool. Javan remembered the old man talking about times when you couldn't cook by gas or by some magical means. In that case…Javan rummaged in the cupboards over the grill. He did a few steps from a happy Pingasporean dance when he found neatly cut sticks of wood and, near them, skinny twigs that would do for kindling.

He built the makings of a fire in the bottom of the grill. Then he stopped being happy again. How was he supposed to get it started? No lighter handy—no firestick, either. More rummaging produced a match safe. He'd seen matches a few times, although he couldn't remember ever using one.

Fortunately, the match safe had pictures on the side to show him what to do. He learned by experiment even so: he broke the first match he tried, and burned his fingers with the second one. That pulled some more Pingasporean profanity out of him. The third match went out before he could start the fire with it. On his fourth try, though, the kindling caught. He clapped his hands together and watched in fascination as the flames spread to the bigger sticks.

Then he got to work. The other snack-sellers and helpers started coming in. Some of them started cooking with assurance; others fumbled almost as much as Javan had.

Bordric, unsurprisingly, seemed ready for almost anything The Train might show him. He got his grill started twice as fast as Javan had. "I hate these in-between times," the big, fair man grumbled. "You don't know what the demon's going to work, or whether anything will."

Someone tapped Javan on the shoulder. He jumped and whirled at the same time; he hadn't known anybody was behind him. But there stood Siilo. Without a word, the snack-seller started loading skewers of meat and vegetables onto the tray strapped around his neck.

Javan was miffed. "You would have said plenty if I didn't have them ready for you," he complained.

Siilo looked astonished. "You bet I would! Is your job to have them ready. Your *job*, you understand? Nobody give you gold bracelet just because you do your job. Job is what you supposed to do. You don't do it, I find somebody else who will. I find somebody else plenty quick. You better believe I do."

As soon as he'd filled the tray, he went away. He had his job to do, too, and he was going to do it. Javan stared after him. Little by little, he realized Siilo had paid him a compliment of sorts. If the old man had praised him, what would it have meant? Only that Siilo was surprised he'd done his job. But Siilo wasn't surprised. Siilo expected him to do it. And if Javan did what was expected of him, why get excited about it?

"My job," Javan muttered. The word felt different in Train-talk: somehow weightier than it would have in Pingasporean. "My job," he said again, and fed the fire more wood.

Pretty soon, Javan was cooking over blue flames again. Then The Train passed through another land where magic replaced the mechanical arts. The dragons that drew The Train here were different from the ones in Dongorland: they were squatter, more metallic in color, with bronze wings that seemed too small to bear their weight.

Nor did a smiling salamander heat Javan's grill in Marmorica. No: what might have been a tiny sun blazed there. It went red and cool as the real sun set, and came back to life at dawn. In the nighttime hours, something that might have been a miniature frozen moon chilled the cooler. It went out at sunup, but the cooler held the chill all day.

That tiny sun did what it needed to do, but Javan liked the salamander better. How were you going to make a little sun happy, or a little moon? You couldn't—it was as simple as that.

Bordric maintained that the little sun and moon and other such manifestations of Marmorica weren't true magic at all, but mechanical arts that only the people living in those parts understood and could use. "What about the dragons?" Javan asked.

"What about them?" Bordric said. "For all you know, for all I know, they really are made of metal."

"They eat meat," Javan pointed out. He'd watched them do it. They were neater feeders than the dragons of Dongorland, but they might have been even more thorough: they demolished carcasses bones and all.

"Yes, but who knows how it feeds them? Who but a Marmorican, I mean?" Bordric stuck out his bearded chin and looked stubborn. "When the mechanical arts go far enough, you cannot tell them apart from magic."

"Feh," Javan said: a disgusted noise he'd picked up from a little old man in his carriage who always wore a small, knitted skullcap. "That's a clerk's way of thinking, or a bookkeeper's."

He couldn't get under Bordric's skin. "It's *my* way of thinking," the snack-seller said, flipping meat-filled pasties with a spatula.

Marmorica wasn't as big as Dongorland: or rather, The Railroad didn't pass through so much of it. Pretty soon, Javan was going through the cabinets above the grill, looking for that match safe again. He was proud of himself for getting the first match lit this time. Then, a moment later, he was furious at himself because he burned his hand with it. Firesticks were much more predictable.

He was dicing tubers a few days later when The Train slowed down to load and unload at yet another city's depot. "Kambok!" the conductors called. "This stop is Kambok!"

Javan almost sliced his fingers. He jerked his left hand away from the knife just in time. Siilo came in to fill up his tray a few minutes later. "New people coming on!" he said happily. "They taste what I sell, they keep buying from me as long as they ride!"

All the other snack-sellers were thinking exactly the same thing, of course. The converted freight car was as crowded as Javan had ever seen it. Men and women yelled at one another. But Javan's mind was running on a different track altogether. "I'm going to need to ask something from you," he told Siilo.

"Eh? What's that?" The old man cupped a hand behind his ear to show he hadn't heard.

"I'm going to need to ask something from you," Javan repeated.

Siilo did hear him that time. "Oh, you are, are you?" The snack-seller did his best to sound ominous. "What you want now?"

"Some time off at our next stop," Javan said.

"You think so, do you?" Siilo clapped a hand to his forehead to show his opinion of that. "Why you care even a fart's worth about a nowhere place like Pingaspor?"

A little stiffly—well, more than a little stiffly—Javan answered, "It's my city. It's where I got on. This is The Train's first time back since I got on."

"Oh." A long pause followed. Siilo looked sheepish, an expression Javan wasn't used to seeing on his worn features. At last, he said, "All right. Go ahead. You do. Never mind me. Sometimes I stick my foot in my face so I can find out what it taste like."

"Thank you, Siilo." Javan left it right there. Yes, he could have had a softer boss—Siilo worked him as if he were a device shaped by the mechanical arts. Siilo also worked himself just as hard, or maybe harder. Javan had to take that seriously. And he'd seen he could also have had a rougher boss. The old man hardly ever hit him. When Siilo did, Javan couldn't think of a time he hadn't deserved it. And Siilo didn't hit very hard even when he did hit. Some of the other helpers in the converted freight car weren't so lucky.

From what Luisa said, the serving girls and laundresses had the same kinds of troubles, although they didn't always show up the same way. "Women telling you what to do are bad enough," she told Javan. "They screech at you when you mess up. Sometimes they pull your hair. And you mostly can't get back at them. If they catch you, you lose your job. Maybe they throw you off The Train in the middle of nowhere."

"Bad enough?" Javan echoed when she said that. "The men are worse?"

She beamed at him. "You were listening!" she exclaimed—by the way her voice chimed, she might have announced a miracle.

"I always listen to you, Luisa," Javan had said seriously.

He'd been serious enough to fluster her, in fact, but not serious enough to derail her. "Yes, the men are worse, or some of them are," she said. "They don't scream or slap you around most of the time, but some of them think they can put their hands wherever they want if you make a mistake. If you make a big mistake, some of them expect you to keep them happy so you can stay out of trouble."

"They'd better not expect that kind of thing from you!" Javan's hands had curled into fists. "I'll make them sorry if they do."

"The one I really have to worry about is a woman who likes girls," Luisa said. "But she doesn't like me that way, or she hasn't tried anything if she does like me that way."

"She's foolish not to," Javan said, and that got him kissed.

As The Train pulled into Pingaspor, though, everything that had happened in his journey round the world receded into the background of his thoughts. He pressed his nose up against the glass of his third-class carriage. The familiar look of the people and the familiar look of the skyline brought tears to his eyes. There were the Needle of Victory, the great statue of the Patriot without a Name, the Wisdom Stupa, and so many more buildings he'd taken for granted while he lived here. And there was the bulk of the depot straight ahead. The Train chugged and squealed to a halt.

Javan's nose mashed against the glass harder than ever. His breath clouded it as the air scoops brought smells long familiar but now overlain with others to his nostrils. He stared out avidly across the platform. Had anyone come to see how he was doing? Was anyone he knew getting on The Train?

There was Kiri! Although her breasts remained pert and lovely, he was amazed at how ordinary she seemed to him. It wasn't just because she walked hand-in-hand with chubby, silly Uharto, either—at any rate, Javan told himself it wasn't. What Kiri saw in Uharto, Javan couldn't imagine, but he didn't waste much time worrying about it.

A couple of Pingasporeans did board The Train, but they were both older people, people Javan didn't recognize. The man got into a second-class carriage. The woman went straight into first class. How much silver wire did *that* cost? Not just more than Javan had. Plenty to sink a good-sized boat, unless he missed his guess.

At last, Kiri noticed his face in the window. She pointed at him. Javan waved. Kiri fluttered her fingers back at him, but at the same time she said something to Uharto. They both went into gales of laughter. Through the glass, Javan couldn't hear what she said. He didn't need long to realize that was bound to be just as well.

When a series of little jerks rippled along The Train's couplings and it began to roll out of the Pingaspor depot, Javan fogged the window glass with another sigh. This one was a sigh of relief, not a sigh of longing and homesickness like most of the earlier ones.

Out of the depot went The Train. Javan's view expanded. There was the silver Ocarina. There was that face carved into the distant cliff. Whose face it was, Pingasporeans never tired of arguing about.

And there was Siilo, coming through the cars tirelessly calling his wares. Seeing Javan still looking out the window, the old man with the wispy beard paused long enough to say, "I was maybe wrong. Not such a terrible bad place, Pingaspor. Plenty worse ones along The Railroad, I bet."

"Don't worry about it," Javan said. "If this isn't nowhere, you can sure see it from here."

When The Train left Liho on its way across the rest of the great ocean, Siilo started complaining about how much his ankle bothered him as he went from one carriage to another, walking with his tray from sunup to sundown. Siilo always complained, of course; Javan wouldn't have known what to make of his boss in a cheery mood. And an old man's aches and pains gave Siilo a running start on things to grumble about.

But this felt different. Most of the time, Siilo's grousing meant the same thing as steam hissing out through a safety valve. As long as Siilo groused, as long as the steam hissed out, everything was fine. When silence fell, that was when an explosion might be on the way.

Here, though, Siilo actually had something to complain about. The ankle was swollen; Javan could see as much. Walking on it had to hurt. Walking on it as much as the old man did had to hurt a lot.

Finally, Javan asked him, "Do you want to tend the grill for a while and let me go through the carriages selling the snacks?"

He waited for his boss to cuss him up, down, and sideways. And, sure enough, Siilo puffed up as if he were about to. But then he didn't. Instead, he asked, "You think you know Traintalk good enough?"

"What do you think?" Javan returned. He wasn't perfectly fluent in The Train's stripped-down native tongue, but he got along pretty well.

"Mm…It could be." Siilo found another question: "You think you really able to sell?"

"*Sim.* I do." Javan hoped he sounded confident—more confident than he felt.

Siilo sent him a ferocious glare. "You start costing me, I go back out there my own self and I stick you in front of grill again."

"I already figured that out." Now Javan hoped he sounded calm. If Siilo did order him back to the converted freight car, when would he get another chance to escape it? Not till the old man died, chances were. Maybe not even then. If you couldn't do the work, you hurt not only yourself but everyone else who depended on you.

"Well, all right. We try. We see how you do," Siilo said. "Maybe I get me a stool, so I don't stand on this stupid leg all the time while I cook." When Javan heard that, he realized Siilo wasn't feeling good at all.

He said, "When I go through the carriages, I'll tell them I'm selling Siilo's snacks. That will make them want to buy."

For the first time since he'd proposed going out in Siilo's place, something approaching approval replaced worry on his boss' wrinkled face. "*Sim*, you do that. I was going to tell you to, but you already think of it for yourself. That good. Maybe you lazy, but could be you not stupid."

Javan started to get angry. Showing that would have been a bad mistake. To keep from showing it, he spoke in his driest tones: "Could be."

"Heh." Siilo cuffed him, again more in affection than not—but not altogether. "Besides your brains, you got one other thing going for you when you carry the tray."

"Oh? What's that?" Javan asked, as he knew he should.

"If I do cooking, what you sell will be super extra delicious," Siilo answered proudly.

"Could be," Javan said, his voice as dry as it had been a moment before.

He made the old man laugh out loud. That filled *him* with pride—he could count the times he'd managed it on his fingers.

He'd told Siilo he could sell. He'd told himself the same thing at the same time. He hadn't the faintest idea whether he was telling the truth. Luisa assured him that he'd do fine. Her trust made him feel better and worse at the same time. He would have been crushed if she hadn't thought he could do it. But if he failed now, he'd fail her, too. And that would be more crushing still.

His heart thuttered when Siilo draped the strap to the tray around his neck. The old man had to adjust it so the tray sat right—Javan was half a head taller. He felt proud again once it went into place, as if he were a prince invested with a magic sword in one of the costume dramas that delighted Pingasporeans.

My home city makes up stories about magic. Me, I've seen it, Javan thought. That helped steady him. So did the delicious aromas rising from the tray as Siilo filled it full. Surely no magic sword had ever smelled so good.

Siilo set a callused hand on his shoulder. "Go sell, boy. Go. Keep us both eating. I make more for when you sell all that."

"Not all of it." Javan ate the meat and onions and mushrooms off one skewer in a couple of quick bites. "Breakfast."

"Breakfast," Siilo agreed. "You see how super extra delicious it is when I do it?"

"Oh, yes. You have everything spiced just right." Javan wasn't about to argue with his boss, especially when he didn't have to strain himself to pay a compliment. It wasn't as if Siilo had forgotten what he was up to at the grill just because he'd been away from it for a little while.

Once Javan finished eating, he had no excuses left. If he was going to do this, he had to do it. He took a deep breath and wiggled a little to make the strap more comfortable. Then he walked away from Siilo, through the little vestibule between the converted freight car and the hindmost passenger carriage, and into a kind of chaos different from the one he'd got used to with the snack-sellers and their helpers.

The third-class carriage was packed. Javan had never seen a third-class carriage that wasn't packed. Children yelled and clambered over benches and ran up and down the narrow aisle. One of them almost tripped him as soon as he walked into the carriage.

"You stupid moron, watch where you're going!" the brat squalled in Traintalk. He thought it was Javan's fault!

Javan didn't boot the little monster halfway to the other end of the carriage. His family had trained him to be polite. That was a demon of a lot more than you could say for the horrible kid.

"Snacks! Siilo's snacks! Get your skewers right here!" The first time Javan came out with it, he could hardly hear his own voice. The children, the dicers, the drinkers, the poor people—the people like him—in the carriage would have had no idea he was there if they hadn't seen him and smelled what he was carrying.

"Gimme one of them," a skinny woman said, tugging at his tunic. "And where's Siilo at, anyways?"

"He's cooking for a while," Javan answered as he handed her a skewer. "The food is super extra delicious now." He stole Siilo's line without a qualm.

"That's what you say." The woman gave him a debit card. He did what he needed to do with it and returned it. On this stretch of The Railroad, the mechanical arts seemed strong, perhaps even stronger than they were in Pingaspor. Pretty soon...*I'll worry about that when The Train comes to it*, Javan thought. *Not like I don't have plenty of other things to worry about now.*

He went up through the third-class carriages, calling, "Siilo's super extra delicious snacks! Get Siilo's super extra delicious snacks right here!"

He made sales. The tray emptied. People were used to buying Siilo's snacks. They'd buy them from someone else, as long as that someone else made it plain what they were. A lot of them would, anyhow.

Before long, Javan had to go back to the grill to fill up the tray. Sure enough, Siilo had snagged a tall stool from somewhere. Maybe it was a discard from a saloon car; it wobbled to and fro as The Train rolled along the track. Siilo rode it with as much aplomb as if he'd perched on it for half his life.

"You back already?" he barked at Javan. "I bet you eat up half the tray yourself, and that's how come."

"No such thing," Javan said indignantly. "Here. See for yourself." He showed Siilo the numbers on the card-reader.

"Huh." The old man shoved it away. "Don't you stand around here, all oopy-doopy on account of you sell maybe a little bit. Go do some more." He started filling Javan's tray again.

"Oopy-doopy?" That was a bit of Traintalk—if it was Traintalk—Javan had never heard before.

"Oopy-doopy." Siilo sounded sure of it. But then, Siilo sounded sure of just about everything. "Go on now. Get out of here. Work!"

Because he'd just gone through the third-class carriages, Javan didn't sell much in them in his second pass. He wasn't too upset at that; he'd known it would happen. So he took the tray up to the second-class carriages.

He hadn't been up there since he boarded The Train. He sometimes thought he'd barely been up to the third-class carriages since he started working for Siilo; he'd spent most of his time on that smooth wooden bench either sleeping or trying to sleep.

Second class was a different world, as different from third as Dongorland was from Pingaspor. Second class seemed as magical as that now-approaching land of sorcery, too. The aisle was wider. The individual seats seemed wide, too, and generously padded. They were also generously spaced. They went back if you wanted to sleep in them, or even if you just wanted to relax. There was carpet under his sandals when he walked up through these carriages.

Would anyone here want to buy from him? Only one way to find out. "Siilo's snacks!" he called, nervously at first but then with more energy in his voice. "Siilo's super extra delicious snacks!"

"Give me two skewers," a man said, holding up his thumb and forefinger in case Javan didn't understand him. "Where's the old man?"

"He's cooking for a while," Javan answered. "That's why the snacks are super extra delicious."

"I liked 'em fine before," the man said. Hearing that made Javan feel good, since he'd cooked them before. He'd done it to Siilo's recipe, of course, but the work was his own. The customer went on, "I've seen how his leg was bothering him. Is that why you're doing the carrying for now?"

"It is," Javan said. "Let me have your card, please."

"Here you go." The man handed it to him. "When you go back there, tell him Minifing hopes he feels better soon."

"Minifing." Javan repeated the name so he wouldn't forget it. "I'll do that."

"Thanks." Minifing nodded. "He knows who I am. I've been buying from him for a long time." He sounded pleased that Siilo would recognize his name. "His food is cheaper than what you can get in the dining cars. You ask me, it's better, too. Some people don't care how they spend their money. I'm stupid all kinds of ways, but not like that."

"Good for you. Me, neither," Javan said.

Minifing chuckled at that. "Oh, I believe you, son. Siilo wouldn't take on anybody who was. He's stupid some ways, too, but not like that. And me...I started out back there on those lousy hard benches myself, you know. I remember what that was like—you bet I do. This here, this is better."

Sitting soft? Sleeping soft? Sleeping stretched out? The only trouble with coming up here was that Javan envied the people who got to stay here all the time. It felt cooler here than it did in the third-class carriages, too, or maybe just more reliably cool. Whatever they used in the carriages where Javan usually stayed, sometimes it worked and sometimes it didn't. No, third class wasn't everything it might have been—not even close.

"Don't waste all your time gabbing with Minifing," a woman a couple of rows farther up called to Javan. "I want to get something to eat, too."

"He's not wasting his time, Rosita," Minifing said with dignity. "He's spending it." Rosita made a rude noise. Minifing laughed.

So did Javan, more from relief than for any other reason. The people in the second-class carriages had more money than he did. Well, all right—lots of people in Pingaspor had had more money than he did, too. But even the richer Pingasporeans *were* people. And the same seemed true of these second-class passengers.

Javan sold Rosita her skewers. He made his way up the aisle. "Siilo's snacks!" Now he sounded like himself. "Siilo's super extra delicious snacks! Get 'em here! Get 'em from me! Get 'em now!"

Damned if they didn't. They weren't just people of a familiar sort. They were *hungry* people of a familiar sort—the best kind of people, as far as a snack-seller was concerned. And, because they had more money, they bought more food. Javan also liked that.

Quite a few of them asked after Siilo. Javan hoped he got all their names right. If he didn't, the old man would likely give him a hard time when he brought them back to the converted freight car.

Siilo, in fact, proved more interested in the numbers on the card-reader than in the customers' best wishes. He liked them, yes, but in the same way a sausage-maker liked his hogs. However much he liked them, he had to extract value from them. That came before everything else.

He plucked a white hair from his chin beard. His eyes crossed as he looked at it. Then he let it fall. "Well," he said at last. "I have worse mornings myself sometimes, bugger me blind if I don't."

"The snacks must be super extra delicious," Javan said, deadpan.

"*Sim.* I bet that's it," Siilo answered. "Now they getting hungry for lunch. You go out again. Could be you work all the way up to first-class carriages. That don't happen every day. You bet it don't—not even close."

In all the time Javan had traveled on The Train, he'd never once set foot in a first-class carriage. He had an idea of how much it cost to travel in that kind of style. Plenty more than the likes of him had, that was how much. He counted himself lucky that he'd been able to get on The Train at all.

Minifing had started off in the third-class carriages, though. He'd said so. Somehow, he'd managed to put enough together to upgrade his ticket. Javan was used to his bench by now. He wondered if he'd still be able to fall asleep stretched out on something soft.

He sighed. Finding out would be nice, wouldn't it?

Siilo's glare snapped him out of his reverie. "How come you still hanging around?" the old man growled. "Go on. Go sell. Super extra delicious!"

Javan made himself nod. "Super extra delicious. Right." And away he went.

The conductor studied Javan's ticket. He also studied the bits of silver wire Javan had pressed into his hand. At last he nodded, with deliberation a judge might have admired. "We can make that change," he said, as solemnly as that judge might have pronounced guilt or innocence in a capital case.

"Then do it, please," Javan said.

"All right. I do it." The conductor used Traintalk with some of Siilo's abruptness. He wrote on the ticket. He punched it with a brass punch. And he stamped it with the seal ring he wore on his right middle finger. The stamp glowed for a moment with a clear blue light—they were in Marmorica, and magic played its part in everything they did. Smiling, the conductor looked from Javan to Luisa, who stood beside him. "This suits you, young lady?"

"Oh, yes!" Luisa's hand stole into Javan's. He squeezed. She squeezed back.

"Well, good. It had better. People get seats side by side, they need to get along, you know?" the conductor said.

Javan squeezed Luisa's hand again. "We wouldn't have changed seats this way if we didn't," he said. She nodded.

And his reply was nothing but the truth. Yes, he'd had to pay a fee to The Railroad to change his seat to the one next to Luisa's. He'd also had to pay the man who'd been sitting beside her to trade seats with him. He hoped the middle-aged woman from Kambok wouldn't be too sorry at getting a new seatmate—she'd always been kind to him. He also hoped she didn't feel like going to the saloon car and hoisting a few to celebrate getting rid of Javan at last. He didn't think she would, but you never could tell.

"All right." The conductor leered. "Third class. Everybody see everything that happen in third class. Everybody gossip about it, too. Even in the middle of the night, everybody see. You know someplace quiet you can go?"

Luisa looked down at the hardwood planks on the floor. She wasn't pale-skinned like Bordric, but her ears turned pink anyhow. Javan wondered if the conductor wanted to tell them about a discreet, quiet place or two—for some more silver wire, of course. Instead of finding out, he said, "I think we'll manage."

"Well!" The man in the blue kepi threw his hands in the air. Yes, he'd been angling for another fee, one that would go straight into his pocket, not to The Railroad. "I hope you do." The way he said it made him out to be a liar. Muttering under his breath, he stomped off.

"Someplace quiet." Luisa smiled saucily at Javan. "*Sim*, I think we can find a place like that. If we were up in first class..."

"Wish for the moons while you're at it," Javan said. Now he'd sold snacks up in first class. He knew what it was like. They didn't just have reclining seats there. They had real beds, and curtains you could pull around them. He hadn't seen any hired pretty girls or handsome men sharing those beds with the first-class passengers, but that didn't mean there weren't any. Behind those curtains, you could do whatever you wanted, and no one would ever know—unless you made too much noise, of course.

Now he also knew exactly what riding up there cost. It wasn't enough to buy The Train. (He didn't think so, anyway.) But it was a lot more than a young snack-seller with a brand-new spouse who served meals in the dining car could readily imagine having. He wished he were rich. Wishing didn't seem likely to make it happen, even in a land where magic worked.

Sure enough, though, he and Luisa did know some spots that were quiet, at least in the middle of the night. It might have been more comfortable in a nice, soft bed, but it was wonderful any which way. While Javan held Luisa, he thought he was richer than all the first-class passengers put together.

Then he'd grab what sleep he could, and then he'd go back to work for Siilo. No one who worked for Siilo was ever likely to imagine he was rich—not for long, he wasn't. Rich or not, though, Javan was happier than he could ever remember being.

Around the world. West to east. No matter what the people riding on it did, no matter what they loaded onto it or took off it, The Train rolled on. A little less than a year after Javan found his place in that third-class carriage, it slowed to a stop in Pingaspor for the second time.

As he had before, he begged some time off from Siilo and jammed his face up against the window glass to get a look at his home city. He'd changed a lot since coming aboard. He was still only beginning to realize how much (for that matter, he was still changing, too). He'd found steady work—maybe not work he wanted to do for the rest of his life, but work that kept him fed and kept him busy. And he'd found love.

Pingaspor had also changed. Not for the better, either, or it didn't seem so to him. The streets of his home city had always been packed with cycles and segways®, buses and trucks, hoppers and people on foot. Now they looked eerily empty.

No—almost empty. Here came a long column of soldiers. Under the beetling brims of their fritzhats, their faces, all slabs and angles and impassive eyes, might have been machined from bronze. They carried firespears and storm rifles and marched in perfect unison, again like machines.

The city rulers had slapped posters on everything that didn't march. The posters that didn't shout about how wonderful Pingaspor was did shout about how awful and wicked and vile and perfidious Namila was.

"But that's silly!" Javan exclaimed. The next city farther east was just the next city farther east...wasn't it? Was he suddenly supposed to think Luisa was awful and wicked and vile and perfidious? She came from Namila. He remembered when she'd got on The Train, right after he had. "Silly," he said again. He loved her no matter where she came from.

Nobody in Pingaspor seemed to think all the insults the locals were flinging at Namila were silly. Or if people did, they didn't dare show it, for fear of what the rulers would do to them. Javan didn't think he'd ever seen anyone so much in earnest as those soldiers.

When The Train reached the depot, the platform was almost empty. Javan had wondered if he'd be able to spot Kiri and Uharto in the usual jostling crowd, but there was no crowd. More soldiers in their tarncapes made sure of that. A few somber passengers waited to get on. Stevedores stood by to deal with freight. And that was about it.

"Pingaspor!" the conductor shouted in several tongues as The Train slowed to a stop. "All out for Pingaspor!" Did they sound less sure of themselves than usual, as if wondering why anybody in his right mind would want to get off at Pingaspor today? It might have been Javan's imagination, but he didn't think so.

Two or three people did disembark. They stood on the platform with dazed expressions, as if wondering what they were going to do in a city that might have taken leave of its senses. No, not *as if*—that had to be exactly what they were wondering. And the new passengers, the ones escaping Pingaspor, jumped onto The Train with the air of folk who knew they were escaping by the skin of their teeth.

One of them carrying his scanty belongings in a flowery carpetbag came through the carriage from which Javan was watching. "What's going on there, friend?" Javan asked him.

Pingasporean felt strange in his mouth; he'd started getting used to Traintalk.

The man was so new to The Train that he didn't know enough to be surprised at hearing his own language. He rolled his eyes. "What's going on?" he said. "The Namilans are thieves, that's what. They're thieves, and our rulers are robbers. And I'm out of all the mess, and I'm the luckiest man in the world because I am."

That didn't make much sense. Javan wanted to ask him more, but the new passenger was hurriedly pushing down the aisle, looking for his seat. And thumps and bumps from farther back announced that the freight cars were already closing up. The handlers didn't usually work so fast. They had to want to clear out of Pingaspor, too.

Out of Pingaspor The Train went—ahead of schedule, which was a prodigy. As Javan walked through the carriages hawking Siilo's snacks, he kept sneaking glances out the window. He saw more columns of soldiers, some on foot, some in trucks, moving steadily east, toward the border with Namila. He also saw things that had to be weapons: weapons he hadn't dreamt that Pingaspor owned.

A few of the people in the carriages also looked out at the advancing soldiers. Most passengers simply ignored the spectacle. Even most of the ones who did look took it as entertainment, as pageantry, not as anything that might prove important to them.

Javan wished he could feel the same way. He might well have felt like that, had his home city not been involved. He kept wondering if he would recognize any of the soldiers. He didn't. Going into uniform made them all look alike to him.

"It's just…out there," said a man in a second-class carriage as they rolled past more men in fritzhats and tarncapes. "It can't have anything to do with us. After all, we're on The Train."

"That's right," the sleek woman across the aisle from him agreed. The rest of the passengers in the carriage who heard them—and who cared—nodded. Javan hoped the man was right, too. Who wouldn't?

Back in the converted freight car, though, Siilo looked and sounded worried. "Could be bad," he said, taking meat off the grills with his tongs. "Could be very bad. I remember when I was maybe younger than you—"

"A long time ago," Javan broke in.

"*Sim.* A long time ago." If Javan had tried to get Siilo's goat—and he had—he hadn't succeeded. Siilo knew he wasn't young any more. How could he not? He went on, "I was just on The Train. There was a big fight between two cities way over on the far side of the ocean. *Big* fight. Schedule didn't come back together for a *looong* time." He gave the word a mournful stretch.

"You think that will happen here?" Javan asked. "A war…" His voice trailed away. He couldn't remember the last time Pingaspor had fought a war. Nobody alive now in the city could. That might have been why the rulers seemed so eager to start one.

Siilo's narrow shoulders went up and down in a shrug. "What do I know? Not *my* city." His tone mocked the way Javan had begged him for time off to get another look at Pingaspor. He aimed a bony forefinger at Javan's chest as if it were a firespear. "Is *your* city. They crazy enough here to want big fight?"

"I didn't think so," Javan said slowly. "But it does look that way, doesn't it?"

"Sure does." Siilo whistled tunelessly between his teeth. He managed a smile, even if it looked forced. "All moonsshine, I hope. Anyway, pretty soon we be gone. We don't got to worry about it then."

"True!" Javan was ashamed of the relief he heard in his own voice. That he was ashamed of it didn't mean it wasn't there.

"So in the meantime, you go on and sell super extra delicious snacks. What else can you do?" Siilo raised a sly eyebrow.

"Unless you want to hop off, put on uniform your own self, and start burning up young men from next city?"

"No, thanks!" Javan heaped the tray high with snacks and got out of there as fast as he could.

He wasn't too quick to miss Siilo's murmured, "No, you not so dumb." Whether it made him feel better or worse or both at once he couldn't have said.

It was all foolishness to Luisa. "Namila couldn't have done anything bad enough to make Pingaspor want to start killing people," she said.

Javan wondered whether Namila had started killing people first. He had sense enough not to say that when he didn't know one way or the other; he was learning. What he did say was, "It hasn't got anything to do with you and me. It hasn't got anything to do with The Train, either."

Luisa thought about that for a little while. Then she leaned toward him on their third-class bench and gave him a kiss. He'd never been happier than he was when she did. "Good for you," she said. "Why did we come aboard, if it wasn't to get away from such stupid stuff?"

Right then, Javan couldn't have said why he'd boarded The Train. He just knew he had. He also knew that, even if soldiers were moving out there in the nighttime, he'd worked hard all day. He felt it from the soles of his feet to the roots of his hair.

He started to say something else to Luisa, but yawned instead. He waited for her to laugh at him. Only a soft snore came from her. He wasn't the only one who'd worked hard all day. Soon, his head cradled in the hollow of her shoulder, he fell asleep, too.

The whistle screamed in the middle of the night. The Train's brakes screamed, too. Javan and Luisa almost tumbled off the bench. "Emergency stop!" somebody shouted.

"Think so, do you?" someone else asked—someone with the aplomb to stay sarcastic in the middle of, well, an emergency stop. With babies wailing, children shrilling, and men and women crying out in what must have been half a dozen different languages, that wasn't easy.

What would have happened if we didn't stop fast enough? Javan wondered. *How close did it come to happening anyhow?* Those were good questions, weren't they? Javan was just as glad not to have good answers to them.

He looked out through the window. Nothing—it was as dark out there as if they were going through a tunnel under the mountains. Darker, in fact: in the tunnel, they had dim lamps every so often.

And then, all of a sudden, it wasn't dark any more for a little while. Something not nearly far enough away exploded, filling the halted carriage with harsh orange light. The children who hadn't shrieked up till then all started at once. More than a few men and women shrieked with them. The roar of that enormous blast did its best to drown all the shrieks, and its best seemed much too good to Javan.

He couldn't have said why he didn't start screaming himself. He might have been too scared to let out even a peep. Or he might not have wanted to show Luisa he was afraid. Later, it occurred to him that she must have had a pretty good idea of that—which had nothing to do with how he acted in the moment.

Darkness slammed down again after the explosion. But it wasn't darkness absolute, the way it had been before. A smaller blaze still burned to mark where the explosion had gone off. And there were other little flames in the night: tongues of red from firespears and storm rifles' golden muzzle flashes.

More booms shook the windows and made everyone shudder. These were farther away than the first one, so the flashes that went with them didn't light up the carriage as savagely. All the same, Luisa asked, "What happens if one of those horrible things comes down on The Train?"

Javan didn't know, not in any detail. "Nothing good," he said. Some questions, you didn't need answered in detail.

"I want to get off!" somebody shouted. Javan didn't. He figured he was safer on The Train than he would be off it.

Everyone the world around knew what The Train was. No one hurt it on purpose. If you were stupid enough to get off in the middle of a war…Anything could happen to you then, anything at all. It could, and it probably would.

Boom. *Boom!* Boom. ***Boomety-boomety-boom!*** The explosions went on and on. Some nearer, some farther away. Some so soft they were barely there. Some louder than anything had any business being.

"I'll never go to sleep in this," Luisa said.

"I know. I was thinking the same thing," Javan answered.

"How long do you think we'll stay stuck here?" she asked.

He spread his hands, palms up. "No way to guess. We stopped so fast…I just hope nothing's happened to The Railroad. If the tracks are hurt, we *can't* go anywhere till they get fixed."

"That would be awful. The schedule—" Luisa broke off. Some things were bigger than The Train and the schedule. Not many, but some. And war, cursed war, was one of those things. Javan had already realized that. Now it was hitting his spouse, too. In a smaller voice, Luisa said, "What happens if we're stuck so long we start running out of food?"

They'd start getting hungry pretty soon. The Train took on supplies at every stop. It was a city in its own right: not a big city, maybe, but a city. "We'll have to get something from somewhere," Javan said slowly.

"From where? How?" Luisa asked.

"I don't know. Somebody will have to take care of it—and no, I don't know who, either," Javan said. "Right now, the best I can do is hope we don't get killed before we find out."

She didn't ask him any more questions for the rest of the night.

They didn't get killed before the sun rose. Nothing the Pingasporeans and Namilans threw at each other came down on The Train. Whether that was good weapon design or merely good luck, Javan couldn't have said.

As soon as it started getting light outside, he went back to the converted freight car. He wasn't surprised to find Siilo there ahead of him. The snack-seller's face couldn't have been longer. "Soon as I cook up what we got in the cold box, we done," Siilo said. "Cooks won't sell me no more. They say they can't get no more. How they sell what they can't get?"

"Well." Javan startled himself: the word sounded like a complete sentence. He found himself continuing, "Let me go outside and see how bad things are."

"If things good, we be moving," Siilo said accurately. "Besides, you go outside, somebody burn you up with a firespear."

Javan remembered what he'd thought of the man who'd wanted to get off the night before. All the same, he said, "I'll be fine if I stay close to The Railroad," and hoped he was right.

"Be careful of soldiers," Siilo said.

"I can talk to them," Javan reminded him.

Siilo snorted. "Be careful anyhow. Who says they listen?"

With that thought to cheer him, Javan did get off The Train and walk up toward the locomotive. A few other passengers were looking around out there, or sketching or photographing the craters that marred the jungle to either side of The Railroad.

And another crater had twisted and melted the tracks just a short spit in front of the engine. If The Train hadn't made that emergency stop, it would have derailed. How many carriages would have flipped over? How many passengers would have got hurt? Or killed?

Something roared by overhead, low, low, low. Rockets fell from under its wings. They flew with minds and fires of their own. When they burst, fresh craters scarred the undergrowth.

A soldier came out of the bushes. Even after he did, his tarncape and the green and brown paint he'd smeared on his face made him hard to see. "You stupid idiots!" he yelled in Pingasporean, and gestured with his storm rifle. "Go back inside where you belong, before you get shot!"

"What's he mooing about?" a passenger who knew no Pingasporean asked in Traintalk.

"He says we'll be safer inside The Train," Javan answered: a true but flavorless rendition.

"He's got his nerve! I am an important personage. How dare he tell me what to do?" the other passenger said indignantly.

"He has a storm rifle. He dares," Javan said. If the other passenger didn't get that, in short order he'd be too dead to worry about anything else. For a wonder, he did. He jumped back aboard The Train as if a dragon were chasing him. Or maybe he found the soldier in the tarncape and the face paint more frightening still. After all, he would have seen dragons before.

Javan got back on The Train, too. He went down to the converted freight car and told Siilo what he'd seen. The old man whuffled out air through his thin, scraggly mustache. "Not good. Very not good. We not go anywhere for a while, right?"

"Sure doesn't look that way," Javan said.

"How we going to eat? I done cook up everything I got. Pretty soon, dining cars done cook up everything they got. What we eat then? Our socks? Some of us don't even got socks."

Luisa had said the same thing. As he had with her, Javan answered, "Somebody will take care of it."

"Somebody!" Siilo stopped whuffling and made a gross, rude noise. "Who?"

When he was talking with Luisa, Javan had had no idea who that somebody might be. Since then, he'd had time to look around, and also time to think. All the same, his breath sighed out before he said, "Maybe me."

"You? You!" Siilo started to laugh. He started to, but he didn't finish. His eyes narrowed, deepening the deltas of wrinkles at their outer corners. He was a crafty old man, all right. "Maybe you." He sounded thoughtful, musing. "You a Pingasporean your own self, sure enough. You can talk with these soldiers, right?"

"I can talk, yes," Javan answered. "Like you said before, though, the only thing that worries me is whether they'll listen."

Siilo smiled a crooked smile. "Show them money. Everybody listen to money. Oh, you bet! Money talk loud, talk plainer even than Traintalk."

"I suppose," said Javan, who wasn't so sure. And he had his reasons, too: "But does it talk louder and plainer than firespears?"

"It can," Siilo said. With that, Javan had to be content. Then Siilo added, "You don't spend your own money for this. You buying for me, so I can keep going." He gave Javan more silver wire than the young man had thought he would get. "Do best you can with it. Try not to get killed."

Out Javan went. Along with the money, he carried his ticket. Without it, he knew he would have been one of those chillingly anonymous Pingasporean soldiers. He could use it to show men who were soldiers why he wasn't one…again, if they felt like paying attention.

The air was hot and sticky. The smells seemed familiar and strange at the same time: familiar because he'd grown up with them, strange because lately he'd fallen out of being used to them. He wondered how far from The Railroad he'd have to go to find a farm. Belatedly, he also wondered whether the soldiers would already have stripped it bare.

Too late to worry about that now. He had to hope they wouldn't have. He also had to hope they wouldn't shoot him or conscript him for the fun of it. Not all the sweat rivering down his face had to do with the heat.

He followed the first little path he found. Guns rattled and explosions thundered off to the east. Did that mean the men from his city were advancing against the Namilans? It meant nothing was exploding by The Train right this minute. Javan approved of that.

"Halt!" a rough voice barked. "Hands up!"

Javan raised his hands. He didn't see the Pingasporean soldier till the man moved. Then he spied the storm rifle pointing straight at his midriff. He stood very still.

The soldier stared at him, eyes wide in a painted face. "What are you doing in that crazy getup, man?" he said. "Asking to get killed?"

"I'm off The Train." Javan pointed back to it without lowering his left hand. "I'm trying to buy some food. We're getting hungry in there."

"You talk just like me," the soldier said suspiciously. "Maybe you're trying to run away from the front and you worked out this dumb stunt to fool us. If you're off The Train, you'll have a ticket, won't you?" He sounded proud of his own cleverness.

"I do have a ticket. Can I show it to you?" Javan didn't reach for it till the soldier grudgingly nodded. Then he held it out to the man from his city.

The soldier snatched it, studied it, and, to Javan's vast relief, handed it back. "I don't want to decide. If I screw up, I'll get it bad. So I'm gonna take you to my captain. Let him figure it out." He gestured with the storm rifle. "C'mon."

Come Javan did. His nose caught a new smell. For a moment, he thought a failed cold box stood open somewhere nearby. Then, gulping, he realized that was the smell of death.

When they finally found him, the captain proved to be a short, chunky man. For a moment, that was all Javan saw. But then the features masked by face paint started to look familiar. "Uharto!" he blurted.

"Javan!" Uharto sounded as surprised as Javan. "What are you doing here? You were on The Train."

"I *am* on The Train," Javan agreed, and pointed back towards it. As he had with the soldier who'd captured him, he explained why he'd got off. After he finished, he took a chance and asked, "How's Kiri doing?"

"She's fine," Uharto answered automatically. Then he drew himself up to his full height, such as it was. "She's going to have a baby—my baby."

"Good for her! Good for you!" If Javan hadn't found Luisa, he never would have been able to bring that out so quickly and naturally. But he had, and so he could.

Afterwards, he saw that the honest congratulations helped tip Uharto his way. The officer's teeth gleamed in his darkened face as he smiled. "Thank you, Javan," he said. He scribbled in a pad, handed the sheet to Javan, and then turned to the soldier who'd brought his acquaintance to him. "I'm giving him a safe-conduct. You help him get whatever he needs, Hanouk. Bad enough The Train's stuck here, but that's the cursed Namilans' fault. But we don't want The Railroad pissed off at us, too."

"Yes, Captain!" The soldier—Hanouk—saluted smartly. Now that he'd been told what to do, he would do it as well as he could. To Javan, he said, "Come on with me. We'll get you stuff, all right. I know where there's a buffalo that needs slaughtering, I do."

The farmer who owned the buffalo seemed astonished to get paid for killing it. (Hanouk seemed astonished that Javan should pay him, too.) The buffalo...Well, no one asked the buffalo's opinion.

Several soldiers helped Javan carry the meat back to The Train. They stared at the carriages in undisguised curiosity. "You were—you are—riding on it?" one of them asked.

"I sure am," Javan said.

"How lucky is that?" the soldier said to his buddies. They nodded. Most of the time, Javan wasn't sure riding The Train was better than staying where he'd been born. Different, certainly. Better was less obvious. Not during a war. He knew when he was well off, and knew better than to rub the soldiers' noses in it.

Siilo cut capers in front of his grill when Javan came back with the roughly butchered buffalo meat. It was more than he could cook up himself. In a low voice, he asked Javan what it had cost. As soon as he knew, he sold some of it to the other snack-sellers. He didn't lose money on the deals—oh, no! They paid without hesitation: it was pay or have nothing to sell.

"Even the dining car pay me for meat soon! Meat and vegetables and what all you can get!" Siilo kissed Javan on the cheek. "Dining car pay *me*! That never happen before."

"Um…" Almost getting shot left Javan less worried about standing up to his boss than he might have been otherwise. After that momentary pause, he plunged ahead: "Some of what you make comes to me. I'm the one who's taking the chances, after all. If I don't get what I deserve, why should I bother?"

"Don't you worry. I treat you square, I promise," Siilo said.

"All right." Javan nodded—it was. Siilo was a rogue all kinds of ways, but when he gave his word he kept it.

He also must have realized that Javan was going to make money for bringing back food any which way. It wasn't long before Bordric sidled up to Javan, silver wire in his big fist. "Here, kid. Get what you can for me, too, will you?"

"I'll try." Javan wondered how far Uharto's safe-conduct would stretch. He was going to find out.

It worked fine for the first day and a half. More snack-sellers than Bordric alone entrusted their money to him. He warned them he was going to charge a commission on anything he got for them. They grumbled, but they couldn't really pretend to be surprised. Sighing, one of them said, "I'll just bump up prices to the passengers. If I haven't got anything to sell, I can't do that. And I guess you aren't in this for your health."

Javan wondered about that health when a squad of soldiers tramped up to him while he was haggling with a tuber farmer. He was getting tired of having deadly weapons aimed at his midsection. Telling that to the men holding those weapons struck him as unwise.

"You are Javan," said the corporal in charge of the squad. The rank badge on his tarncape was almost impossible to see, much less read. The authority he wore was more easily visible.

"I am," Javan agreed.

"Come with us," the corporal said. In case Javan had any hopes of finishing his dicker, the underofficer killed them with one more word: "Now."

Go with them Javan did. They brought him to a colonel. The middle-aged man studied the document Uharto had given him. Then he said, "We have a prisoner here. Do you know him?"

At his gesture, more soldiers led out a very unhappy man in The Train's blue livery, hands cuffed behind his back. Javan said, "His name is Manolis. He works in the dining cars."

"Thank you, Javan!" Manolis exclaimed in halting Pingasporean. "I was only trying to—"

"Shut up," the colonel said flatly, and Manolis did. The colonel went on, "He did claim he was trying to buy food for those people. But he speaks our language so badly, I thought he might be a Namilan spy."

Beaky-nosed, heavily bearded Manolis looked more like a Namilan than an onion did, but not a whole lot more. Javan started to say so. The soldiers' firespears and storm rifles gave him second thoughts. He contented himself with, "He does travel on The Train. He's been on longer than I have."

"If you vouch for him..." The colonel made a sour face. He'd wanted to be a spy-catching hero, maybe a spy-killing hero. He turned to Manolis. "Go back to The Train. Stay on it. If we find you again, you will not have the chance to make any more stupid mistakes. Do you follow me?"

Manolis nodded, but he asked, "How I get things to eat for passengers?"

The colonel pointed to Javan. "Get them through him. He already has a safe-conduct from our military, and he speaks Pingasporean better than a funny-looking monkey like you. Do you understand *that*?"

Something in Manolis' jade-green eyes said he understood it entirely too well. However angry he might be, though, he couldn't do anything about it. He gave another tight-lipped nod. The colonel ordered his hands freed and told off soldiers to take him and Javan back to The Train.

Manolis started swearing in Traintalk on the way there. The corporal who'd seized Javan shut him up sharply: "Talk so I can know what you're saying." Manolis kept as quiet as a tomb till they were aboard once more.

Then he let himself go for a minute or two, in Traintalk and a gurgling language he'd probably grown up speaking. When he ran down, he went back to Traintalk: "Not your fault, Javan. You saved my backside there. The dining cars will buy through you."

As he had with the other snack-sellers, Javan warned, "I'm going to take a cut on the deals."

"I should hope so! I sure would," Manolis said. "As long as you don't screw us too hard, how can we complain?"

"All right. I just wanted to make sure you understood." Javan didn't stay on The Train any longer than he had to. That tuber farmer was eager to sell. And well he might have been. Javan could give him a better price than he would have got from the Pingasporean soldiers. Javan wouldn't shoot him if he groused about prices, either.

Late that evening, Javan told Siilo about his adventures. The old man hugged himself with glee. "Oh, wonderful!" he said. "Wonderful! Snack-sellers always buy from the dining cars. Where else can we get anything to fix and sell? But now they got to buy from us! They bought from me. Now they buy from you. Give it to 'em good!" A pump of his arm showed how he wanted Javan to give it to them.

"Manolis warned me not to get too greedy," Javan said.

Siilo pumped his arm again. "What he do? What any of those blue-clothes bastards do? They pay, that's what! All on account of two stupid cities go to war!" He cackled like a laying hen.

One of the cities that had gone to war was the one where Javan had been born. He started to remind Siilo of that. But what was the point? Whichever reasons Pingaspor and Namila had found to quarrel about, going to war over them seemed pretty stupid to him, too. Stupid or not, he could take advantage of it in a way he couldn't have if two different cities had started wrangling.

He could, and he did. A lot of silver wire passed through his hands over the next few days. Most of it went to nearby farmers. Some went to the soldiers who still kept an eye on him. But some of it, now, some of it stuck.

Luisa's eyes glowed when he handed her some of what he'd made. "We can do a lot with this," she breathed.

"I know," Javan said. "It's not how I would have wanted to get hold of money, but...." He shrugged. "In Dongorland, it would have been somebody else. It's always somebody, though. It has to be. If it's no one, we all go hungry."

Luisa counted the lengths of silver wire again. "Almost, I will be sorry when they fix The Railroad," she said. "Almost."

The repair crew couldn't come out from Pingaspor. The length of The Train blocked it from the stretch of track that needed repair. Javan's city and Namila had to arrange a truce so a crew could come east from Namila through the lines to do the work. From the gossip Javan heard, neither Namila nor Pingaspor wanted to do that. What they wanted to do was to keep fighting.

But the rest of the cities along The Railroad started screaming at the two warring towns. They all depended on The Train, and they all suffered when the schedule failed. If Namila and Pingaspor ever wanted to do business with those other cities again, The Train had to start rolling.

And so, a white flag flying in front of them, the crew came the wrong way up The Railroad from Namila and went to work. Javan whispered in Luisa's ear. She wasn't the only passenger on The Train from Namila. Of course not—nowhere near. But she was the one who went out first to translate for the repair crew. And she was the one who got paid for doing that. She didn't make as much as Javan was bringing in, but every little bit helped.

"They can't just repair the rails. They have to take them out and replace them—they're good for nothing but scrap metal now," she told Javan. He nodded; that squared with what he'd seen up ahead of The Train. Luisa went on, "And they have to rebuild the roadbed before they can do that. I don't know what kind of weapon Pingaspor used on The Railroad, but it was a bad one."

"How do you know it wasn't something from Namila?" Javan answered. "We're still inside Pingasporean territory, so your people could have been shooting it at mine."

Luisa looked surprised. "I didn't think of that," she said after a moment. "I guess they could have been."

And that was as much as the two of them wrangled over whose city was to blame for what. Javan had an opinion about whose fault it was. No doubt Luisa did, too. They didn't start waving those opinions over their heads. Why bother, when neither one could prove his or her opinion was the only true one? Sometimes—often—not starting an argument in the first place was better than winning one.

Javan could see that. Why couldn't Pingaspor and Namila?

Still flying their flag of truce, the Namilan repair crew headed off to the west, through the lines and back to the city from which they'd come. Now white flags fluttered from every car on The Train. You would think nobody could dare shoot at it as it rolled along the track on its endless journey. You would think so, but you might be wrong. If flags of truce made even one hotheaded soldier not pull the trigger, they were worth their weight in gold.

When the whistle howled and The Train at last began to move again, cheers rang out in every passenger carriage—and in the converted freight car where the snack-sellers worked. Javan joined the cheers. Everyone else would have given him a hard time if he hadn't. He had enough common sense to see that.

He felt a pang even so, though he also had sense enough not to show it. Wars ruined people. Wars could ruin whole cities. Only a few lucky folks came out of wars better off than they'd gone in. He'd been lucky this time, and he didn't know when or if that kind of luck would ever come his way again.

They were getting near the front. He could tell because the explosions in the distance he'd got used to hearing while The Train was stopped weren't so distant again. Some of them seemed tooth-rattlingly close, the way they had right after the emergency stop. Maybe the flags of truce weren't even worth their weight in bedsheets.

Javan was walking through the carriages with a tray of super extra delicious snacks when they passed from Pingasporean-held land to territory that belonged to Namila. All he could see out the windows was devastation. Would whoever finally got to keep this terrain want it after the war was over? Javan knew he wouldn't if he ruled a city.

He asked Siilo for a little time off when The Train came in to the depot at Namila. His boss raised an eyebrow. "You want a good look at city that is enemy?" Siilo asked.

"*Sim*." Javan nodded. "I want to see if they've gone crazy, too."

"Of course they crazy," the old man told him. "How you fight a war if you not crazy?"

But Siilo let him go. Javan realized he hadn't just made money while the war stopped The Train. He'd also built up a much larger store of goodwill than he'd ever enjoyed before. Siilo let him cash in a little of that now.

As he'd seen before, buildings in Namila looked different from the ones in Pingaspor. Namilan uniforms were different from the ones Pingasporeans wore, too. These tarncapes were longer; these fritzhats had a little more flair in the brim. The camouflage mix here had a bit more green and a bit less brown. The posters weren't the same as the ones that shrieked from walls and fences in Pingaspor. They weren't the same, no, but they shrieked just as loud.

Also the same were the relieved looks on the faces of the handful of Namilans who passed their cordon of soldiers to board The Train. They could have marched off in tarncapes to fight with firespears. Many of their friends and relatives would already have done that. They were getting away instead. No wonder they looked relieved.

When Javan went back to work, Siilo caught him and asked a one-word question: "And?"

"And you're right," Javan said sadly. "They're crazy, too."

The old man nodded. "See? What I tell you?"

Javan didn't ask Luisa if she'd had a chance to see what had become of her home city. But when they got together the evening after The Train left the Namilan depot, she seemed uncommonly subdued. If you paid attention, some questions answered themselves.

There was one fight between a Pingasporean who'd boarded just before the war started and a Namilan who'd come aboard right afterwards. After the other passengers in the carriage broke it up, both men acted ashamed of themselves. The rest of the newcomers from the squabbling cities either ignored their opposite numbers or went out of their way to make friends with them. They wanted to forget the war, not to keep it going.

Everyone wanted to forget the war. The cooks and stewards who ran the dining cars certainly did. Before long, they started jacking up what they charged the snack-sellers. If the snack-sellers had to pay more, they'd need to raise their prices. And if they did, more passengers would go to the dining cars instead.

"They're thieves," Bordric said. Javan's head bobbed up and down; he felt the same way. The big man eyed him. That pale gaze was disconcertingly keen. In thoughtful tones, Bordric went on, "They wouldn't have the nerve to play these stupid tricks if you were doing the buying for us, Javan."

"You don't think so?" Javan didn't squeak in amazement, but he came close.

"No. I don't," Bordric answered, his deep voice altogether serious. "How about it, Siilo? If I give him money, do you mind if he buys for me?"

"He take his own cut, bigger than he take from me," Siilo warned.

"*Sim, sim.*" Now Bordric sounded impatient. "Of course he will. He's your baby, not mine—you found him. But don't you figure I'll still do better buying through him than letting the dining-car bandits slice me and dice me?"

"Could be," Siilo allowed. "If they remember anything, could be. But who know for sure?"

"Who knows anything for sure?" Bordric rumbled. "Worth a try, though. If it doesn't work out, how am I worse off?"

The boss steward who haggled with Javan didn't have a long, pointed nose like Bordric's, but he looked down it as if he did. His name was Zulman. "Why should you get any special bargain, young fellow?" he asked scornfully.

"Don't ask me." Javan kept his own voice mild. "Why don't you go and ask Manolis?"

Like most people's, Zulman's skin was too dark to show a flush well, but the way his nostrils flared and his lips narrowed said he would have turned red if he could. "That has nothing to do with anything," he said, sounding chillier than any ice elemental.

"No?" Javan tried his question again: "Why don't you go and ask Manolis?"

Zulman's nostrils flared anew, but in a different way: he snorted through them. "So he can tell me how much you cheated us when the shoes were on your feet?"

"Go ask him," Javan urged once more. "What he'll tell you is, I could've done a lot worse. Siilo sure wanted me to—"

"Why am I not surprised?" Zulman broke in.

Ignoring him, Javan finished, "—but I didn't think it was fair. The way you're gouging us now isn't fair, either. You know it isn't. That's why you don't want to talk with Manolis."

"Don't tell me why I want to do things," Zulman snapped, still in those frigid tones. "Wait here. Don't go anywhere. I'll be back." He heaved his bulk out of his chair—who could imagine a skinny steward or dining-car cook?—and lumbered away. Would he really talk to Manolis or only pretend to? Javan couldn't do anything about it but wait, so he did.

When Zulman returned, he looked even less happy than he had before. Javan wouldn't have believed he could. "Well?" the young man asked.

"Pleh!" Zulman said: a sound of pure disgust. "I suppose, since you snack-sellers whine so much, we may possibly be able to make certain minor adjustments to the revised price structure."

Javan needed to work through that to realize he'd just won. "What kind of adjustments?" he asked cautiously. Was this a halfway victory or the real thing?

Zulman wanted it to be a halfway victory, if that. Javan kept haggling. He kept not getting excited. At last, the boss steward threw his hands in the air. "All right. *All right!*" he said. "You have the old price back. For Siilo and for Bordric, you have it."

"What about other snack-sellers who go through me?" Javan tried to sound as naive as he could. He knew that, if he got a better deal than other people did, they would want to go through him.

Zulman could see the same thing. "If they come late to the dance, they have to pay more for the ticket," he said.

"How much more?" Javan wanted it still to be worthwhile for the others to work through him. The more snack-sellers who used him as their buyer, the more commission he could collect. He and Zulman dickered a while longer. Eventually, he got the boss steward down to a point where he could still make money while charging latecomers less than they would pay buying direct from the dining cars.

"This is only because of what happened during the war. Otherwise..." Zulman pursed up his lips and said "Pleh!" again.

"Fair is fair," Javan said. "The Train needs the dining cars. It needs the snack-sellers, too. We should work together. We shouldn't try to drive each other out of business."

All Zulman said to that was "Pleh!" one more time. But he didn't try to back away from what he'd just agreed to.

Javan took the news back to the converted freight car. Siilo and Bordric both wrung his hand and told him what a clever son of a dog he was. Bordric gave him a knock from a little green bottle Javan had never seen before. It was as fiery as a salamander going down, but warmed him nicely after it exploded in his stomach.

"You going to be rich, boy! Rich, I tell you!" Siilo said. "Who would believe it? A snack-seller, he get rich? No, nobody believe that. But you gonna do it."

"I was lucky," Javan said. "And I'm not rich yet." Whatever was in the little green bottle didn't make him lose all his sense, anyhow.

"You gonna be," Siilo insisted. Bordric nodded—he thought so, too. Javan only shrugged. He didn't care about being rich. Well, no: he did care. But he still had trouble believing a snack-seller, a third-class passenger, could make that kind of jump.

Even so, he was eager to tell Luisa about the arrangement he'd hammered out with Zulman. She hugged him. "That couldn't have been easy," she said. "I know him. He thinks every pig we kill for the cooks is like his own son."

"Who knows? He may be right," Javan answered.

She giggled. "Now I'm going to have to find somebody I can tell that to, somebody who'll spread it around without letting anyone find out who started it." Then she yawned. Javan had noticed she'd been acting more tired than usual the past few days.

He was still full of himself. "If you listen to Bordric and Siilo, I'm going to be rich," he bragged.

"If you listen to Bordric and Siilo, you won't have time to do anything else," Luisa replied tartly. This time, Javan laughed. Before he could rise to the snack-sellers' defense, though, she went on, "This once, I hope they're right. I really do, because I'm going to have a baby."

"You're—" Javan's jaw dropped. He asked a man's age-old stupid question: "Are you sure?"

"As sure as I need to be," Luisa said. "And I'm sure of something else, too."

"What's that?" Javan knew he sounded dazed, but he couldn't help it. A baby! That they would have children one of these days was no surprise. That one of these days should turn out to be this one day...was.

"I don't want to raise a baby in a third-class carriage, not if I can help it," Luisa said. "I know lots of people do it, but I want a child of mine—a child of ours—to have things better than that. Do you think you'll make enough to let us upgrade our tickets by the time the baby comes?"

"I...may," Javan answered after some thought. "It depends on how many other snack-sellers decide to let me buy for them, and on how soon they do it."

"Try to get lots of them to, and as soon as you can," Luisa said. "I don't look forward to sleeping on this hard bench when I'm all bulging, either. The seats in the second-class carriages are a lot more comfortable. You even have the chance to stretch out."

"I know," Javan said automatically. He started laughing again. It was either that or bang his head against the—very hard—back of the bench in front of him. Upgrading not one but two tickets from third class to second..."After we do that, we won't need to worry about getting rich for a while. Quite a while, probably."

"We'll manage," Luisa said. "You work hard, and so do I. We've got each other. We'll have the baby, too. We'll both work even harder for it than we do for ourselves. And what more do we need?"

"Nothing, really." Javan hesitated, but in the end he did continue: "When will we find time to sleep in those nice chairs, though?"

Luisa gave him the look a spouse saves for the times when the other spouse comes out with something uncommonly stupid. "We'll manage," she said once more. In ominous tones, she added, "Won't we?"

"Yes, dear," Javan said, which was always the right answer.

The conductor studied Javan's ticket, and Luisa's, with unusual interest. Light from flitting will-o'-the-wisps glinted off his spectacles—they were in Dongorland. "How about that?" he said. "Not the kind of thing folks ask me about every day."

Javan believed that. More often than not, if you took your seat in a third-class carriage when you got on The Train, you'd stay in third class till you got off or till you died—whichever came first. But, as Minifing had shown Javan when he started hawking Siilo's snacks, you *could* move up if you worked hard and if you caught a few breaks—or more than a few.

Javan and Luisa had both worked hard almost from the moment they'd boarded. If they hadn't, they wouldn't have been able to stay on The Train, even in third class. And the war that hurt both Pingaspor and Namila so badly gave him the break he needed. Even when you got one, you had to be able to use it. Javan had done that, too.

"You know there are fees involved," the conductor said.

"We can pay," Javan answered. They'd still have something left after they did. And only a few stubborn snack-sellers—Darvish and a couple of other old men who didn't like Siilo or anyone who had anything to do with Siilo—weren't buying from the dining car through him now. He didn't like to think of it as getting rich. Getting by: that was better.

The conductor changed the subject (or perhaps he didn't). To Luisa, he said, "Looks to me like you're expecting."

"*Sim*, I am." She nodded.

"Good. That's good." The fellow smiled. "Babies, now, babies ride for free long as they don't need a seat of their own. Sooner or later, though, you'll have to buy a place for the little one. Once it's not so little any more, I mean. That's something else you'll want to think about before you move up to second class."

"We have been thinking about it," Luisa said. There was an understatement; it was one of the things that made Javan wonder whether they ever would find time to sleep once they upgraded to second class. Luisa put the best face on it she could: "We don't have to worry about it right now, though. You said so yourself."

"I guess I did." The conductor admitted what he couldn't very well deny. "All right. We'll take care of this now and the other thing when it comes up. One way or the other, that will work out."

A certain warning—or was it anticipation?—roughened his voice. If Javan and Luisa couldn't pay for their child's second-class ticket when the time came, they and the child would all go back down to third. Working your way up once wasn't easy. Working up a second time would be the next thing to impossible.

For now, though, the couple had what they needed to convert their third-class tickets to those for the carriages farther forward. The conductor took their fees. He took their old tickets and gave them new ones. And he said, "I hope you like what you get."

So do I, Javan thought. He'd grown very used to third-class carriages, no matter how strange and crowded they'd seemed when he first climbed onto The Train. Changing to something new made him suspicious, even if it was supposed to be something better.

But Luisa answered firmly: "I'm sure we will." Her eyes challenged Javan to be anything but sure. He didn't have the nerve.

The conductor escorted them to their new seats. The passengers already in the second-class carriage gave them curious looks. When new people took seats in a carriage, it was almost always at a stop. Almost always, but not this time.

A low buzz of conversation rose. "Isn't that the snack-seller?" somebody said.

"It is!" someone else exclaimed. "Siilo's super extra delicious snacks—that's him."

"What's he doing here, though?" a woman asked. "It looks like he's getting seats in this carriage—him and his lady friend." The last couple of words were vitriol dipped in honey.

A man said, "I don't know how many times she's given me lunch in the dining car."

"Is that all she's given you?" The woman couldn't have been bitchier if she'd tried.

"Shh! They'll hear you," another woman said.

And so they would. Javan and Luisa looked at each other. Javan hadn't expected—this. *I should have*, he realized. Plenty of people in Pingaspor jeered at social climbers. Money could buy places. Buying acceptance was harder, in Pingaspor and evidently on The Train, too. It would come more slowly, if it came at all.

"We're here," Javan whispered to Luisa. "We've got as much right to be here as they do. And if they don't like it, too bad for them." She nodded, but her face was troubled.

Slowly and deliberately, Javan settled into the seat he'd got. It *was* soft—soft enough to surprise his spine, which looked for a hard bench back to rub against it. He found the control that made the seat recline. Sure enough, it did. He couldn't tell whether he liked it or not. Yes, he'd got used to being upright all the time.

Beside him, Luisa was getting acquainted with her new seat, too. "This is good," she said. Maybe she was trying to convince Javan, or maybe herself. After a moment, she spoke with more assurance: "And it will be wonderful when the baby comes."

"Of course." Javan couldn't go far wrong agreeing with her. He wondered if he would get any sleep at all in this unfamiliar seat. He hadn't got much his first night in the third-class carriage. Yes, this *was* better. That would matter later. On the first night, its being different counted more.

It did for him, anyhow. Luisa fell asleep right away, and slept as if someone had drugged her dinner. She'd been doing the same thing in the third-class carriage. A woman there told her you slept as much as you could before you had your baby, because you wouldn't sleep at all afterwards. That made more sense than Javan wished it would have.

He looked out the window. It was dark outside, so there was nothing to see. And then, all of a sudden, there was. Fairies—this was Dongorland, and they couldn't have been anything else—danced in a glowing ring. He stared at them in awe and wonder till The Train rolled on and left them behind.

Javan smiled to himself in slow wonder. When you got on The Train, you saw marvels you wouldn't even have dreamt of before you set out. He glanced over at Luisa. Too bad she hadn't glimpsed the shining, dancing fairies. Then his eyes went from her face, slack-featured now in sleep, to her belly. She had a marvel of her own, growing inside her. What did she need with fairies?

On went The Train. Eventually, it came around to Pingaspor again. The war was still going on. The city looked battered. Something had melted part of the domed roof on the Wisdom Stupa, and the Needle of Victory had fallen over and knocked off the Patriot without a Name's left arm, though the rest of the statue still stood. The few people Javan saw on the streets looked worried and preoccupied. No one got on or off The Train. He couldn't remember that happening before. After The Train pulled out of the depot, he saw that the great cliffside face had lost its nose.

White flags flying all over, The Train slowly passed through the fighting zone. No one damaged The Railroad this time. They entered Namilan territory without any trouble. When they reached the city, it also showed scars. The people there seemed as weary and wary and furtive as the Pingasporeans. A woman got off at the depot. No one boarded there.

"It's so sad," Luisa said.

"So stupid," Javan said.

"That, too," she agreed. Her belly bulged enormously now. "I wish this silly baby would come out."

A few days later, it did. Supported by Javan, Luisa waddled to the first-aid car in front of the caboose. Then he went back to work. No matter what else was going on, that wouldn't keep. He didn't get to see how she was doing till after nightfall. The baby still hadn't come.

"Another couple of hours, I think," the midwife said.

"That's not too long," Javan said.

"Yes, it is!" Luisa snarled. "You got the fun. I have to do the work. You—you *man*, you!"

"This is your first?" the midwife asked. She was middle-aged and plump and very calm. Javan managed a nod. She patted him on the arm. "Don't get upset about anything she says in labor. Sometimes women are a little crazy then."

Luisa called him worse things than a man before the baby was born. It was a girl. They named it Irini. It looked squashed to Javan, but the midwife seemed content.

After Irini joined the world, Luisa seemed to realize Javan wasn't really the enemy after all. "What are you going to do tomorrow?" she asked him. "It's the middle of the night—it's past the middle of the night—and you're still up."

"I'll stagger through. That's why there's tea and coffee." Javan expected he would need about a bathtub's worth to make it to the end of the day. If that was what it took, that was what he'd do.

Stagger through he did. He made several quick trips to the lavatories along with everything else, as the coffee and tea took their revenge. And he drank so much that he had trouble dropping off the next night no matter how tired he was and no matter how far that soft, inviting second-class seat reclined (yes, he was used to it now, and had trouble remembering how he'd ever managed to doze off on the third-class bench).

In another day or two, Luisa and Irini would come up beside him. *How am I supposed to sleep then?* he wondered. *What will I do when I can't?* But the answer to that seemed plain enough. He'd pour down as much tea and coffee as he could hold, and if he had to piss all the time, well, he'd do that, too.

Satisfied that he'd worked everything out, he did fall asleep at last.

When The Train rolled into the depot at Pingaspor again, Irini knew how to smile. She made different noises to show she was unhappy in different ways. Javan and Luisa had taken to remembering things by noting what Irini could do when they happened.

The war was over. The people in the streets of Javan's home city were skinny, but they wore ordinary clothes again. Quite a few of them still carried weapons, though.

Posters proclaimed an end to tyranny. Other posters showed the old city rulers on a gibbet. And still others warned Pingasporeans about the enemies of liberty. They didn't say exactly who those enemies were or how people could recognize them.

"It may be peace, but I don't think it's freedom," Javan remarked to Luisa.

"If peace sticks, freedom may come back with it," she answered. Irini's toothless smile said she thought so, or maybe just that she'd had her linen changed and her bottom powdered a few minutes before. Sighing, Luisa added, "I wonder what Namila's like now."

"We'll find out pretty soon," Javan answered in distracted tones. The Train had passed another poster warning that liberty had foes. The man doing the warning on this one was Colonel Uharto. He'd been Captain Uharto when Javan last dealt with him, and silly Uharto the hanger-on before the fighting started.

I took advantage of the war, Javan thought nervously. *I guess Uharto did, too.* He wondered how the captain—no, the colonel—was doing with Kiri these days. He also wondered whether Uharto still had anything to do with her. A colonel whose face and message showed up on posters was someone who could tell lots of people how high to jump. Men like that had no trouble scooping up women if they wanted to, and a lot of them did.

When he said as much to Luisa, the way her eyebrows jumped reminded him of Siilo. "And you still care about Kiri because…?" she asked pointedly.

"I don't care about her. I just wondered, that's all." Javan backtracked in a hurry. Now that Luisa had got in her jab, she let him do it. They did get on well most of the time, not least because they didn't push quarrels as hard as they might have.

If Kiri had got on The Train then…But she didn't, although a couple of Pingasporeans did. Pingaspor might not be back to normal yet, but it did seem to be heading that way.

So did the city of Namila, when The Train reached that depot. If anything, it seemed closer to normal than Pingaspor did. That made Luisa happy and Javan sad. No one could have been anything but sad about the wide swath of shattered landscape between the one city and the other. Soldiers weren't burning one another into shriveled lumps of charcoal out there any more, but the countryside and the ordinary people who'd lived on it would be a long time recovering. Javan hoped the farmers from whom he'd bought food after the emergency stop were all still safe and well. That was as much as he could do; The Train wouldn't stop now to let him find out.

When The Train did stop for resupply and repair at Liho, on The Railroad's island out in the middle of the ocean, Javan didn't take Luisa and Irini to the Fredarvi eatery. Good though it was, he had other things in mind. He hurried to the victualing office.

He wasn't astonished to find Zulman there ahead of him. The boss steward was talking with an official from The Railroad who wore a blue uniform even more encrusted with gold braid than his was. Seeing Javan walk in the door, Zulman did look surprised, but in no good way. He might have found Javan—or half of Javan—in a mango he was eating.

"What are you doing here?" he growled, as if offended because Javan was anywhere near him.

Speaking to the victualing official rather than to Zulman, Javan said, "I came to see about buying meat and tubers and mushrooms and onions."

"You can't do that!" Zulman said furiously. "No miserable, no-account snack-seller has done that since The Railroad put a girdle around the world all these ages ago."

Still speaking to the official from the victualing office, Javan said, "I buy for almost all the snack-sellers on The Train. If I can get supplies for them straight from The Railroad instead of buying from the dining cars, my guess is that I'll have a lower price."

"And you'll cost the dining cars money!" Yes, Zulman was angry, all right. And he had his reasons. Javan was trying to take a bite out of his profits. What could be more dreadful than that?

"*Sim*, but the snack-sellers and the passengers will do better," Javan said.

"The passengers. The *snack-sellers*!" Zulman rolled his eyes in vast contempt. "The dining cars are part of The Railroad. They count for more than people like you, people who had to pay for their own tickets if they were going to ride The Train."

Javan looked toward the victualing-office official. That worthy blandly looked back. Her face showed none of what she was thinking. "There have been snack-sellers for as long as anyone can remember," Javan said. "The Train needs them. Not everybody can afford to eat in the dining cars all the time. Some passengers can't afford to eat in them at all."

"That's not *my* fault," Zulman said haughtily.

"Where does the blame go, then?" The victualing-office official spoke for the first time since Javan came in. The question was one Javan had hoped she would ask.

Zulman had an answer for it, too: "Why, with the passengers, of course! If they don't have the money to keep themselves fed, they've got no business boarding The Train to begin with."

"There *have* been snack-sellers for a long time," the official said. "This fellow is right about that."

"There haven't been any with the nerve to barge into the victualing office before—that's for sure," Zulman said.

"You've kept us split up, competing against each other," Javan replied. "But now I can speak for all of us but two. And because I can, I can afford to buy in bulk here."

"Just because you can afford to doesn't mean you've got any right to!" The boss steward was as hot as a salamander.

"You do not decide that, Zulman." The victualing-office official, by contrast, sounded as cool as the little office where she worked. "I do, and you had best keep it in mind."

"*Sim*, Pripessa," Zulman said unwillingly. He might not have intended to, but he also gave Javan her name.

She turned her dark, unfathomable gaze on Javan. "How much would you want to buy? What do you propose to pay for it?"

He told her. The price he offered was less than what he was paying Zulman; the boss steward's outraged hiss said he noticed that, too. Well, naturally he would. Javan had to make a lower offer. If he didn't, he wouldn't gain anything from this deal. Javan finished, "After all, we feed the passengers, too, whether the dining cars like it or not."

The dining cars, in the person of Zulman, plainly didn't. "You'd never have the chance to do this if you hadn't started scrounging for your lot while we were stuck during the war."

"Not just for the snack-sellers. For the dining cars, too," Javan said.

"Oh!" For the first time, a hint of warmth showed in the victualing-office official's voice. "You're that fellow—Javan." She said his name as if she were reading it off some report she'd got. And so she must have been, inside her head.

"That's right, Pripessa." Javan used her name, too. "I'm Javan."

"I remember hearing about you and what you were able to do. That was remarkable," she said. A small, scratchy sound followed. For a moment, Javan wondered if mice or mirps were gnawing inside the walls. Then it realized it was Zulman, grinding his teeth. Pripessa went on, "We will try a direct sale to you, as representative of the snack-sellers. We will try it, and see how it goes."

"Pripessa!" Zulman exclaimed. "I protest this—this mistaken decision!"

"You may do that," she answered, her own tones dispassionate again. "In writing, in triplicate, as required by The Railroad's regulations. If your protest is upheld, or if things do not work well with direct sale, we can return to the old system. If things do work well, however, and your protest is on the record, the fact will be noted in your promotion jacket. The regulations cover that, too, as I'm sure you recall."

If you wind up looking like an idiot, we'll treat you like one from now on. Javan needed a moment to work out what she was saying, but he did. Zulman chewed on his lower lip. He wanted to hurt Javan. He didn't want to hurt himself.

"Well, perhaps we can await developments," he said at last, in a voice like ashes.

"That seems sensible," Pripessa said, which meant *You don't have the nerve to stick out your neck, because you know it may get chopped.* She swung her attention back to Javan: "I will need to see that you have what you need to get what you want."

"I have it," Javan said, and showed her he was telling the truth. Not all the money was his, but it didn't need to be. And, even paying a lower price than he had to the dining cars, he'd make more on this deal. That was what happened when you cut out the middlemen.

Cut out, Zulman muttered, "If we were in Dongorland, I'd be certain you magicked her."

"We aren't, and I didn't." After a heartbeat, Javan added, "And being sure isn't the same as being right, either."

Pripessa smiled at that, which made Zulman even more unhappy. Then she gave Javan a brisk nod. "You do have it. I'll order the supplies sent to the snack-sellers' work car immediately."

"Thank you!" Javan said. It didn't seem strong enough in Traintalk, the way swearing didn't. He said it again, this time in Pingasporean. He had no idea whether Pripessa understood his birth-language. He didn't much care, either. The way he said it, the way it sounded, got the message across fine.

"You start out working for me," Siilo said. "Now I working for you. Bordric, he working for you. The rest of the snack-sellers, they all working for you, too. How that happen?"

"Not all of them," Javan said. Such talk embarrassed him. He didn't like thinking of it in those terms.

Siilo waved aside the protest. "All who matter. The others—" He made as if to spit. The couple of snack-sellers who still wouldn't buy through Javan balked because they had old grudges against Siilo. Well, he didn't get along with them, either.

"I've been lucky," Javan said.

"Lucky?" Siilo shook his head. "You see luck, you got to run with it. Otherwise, it don't help you none. All this happen in Dongorland, people say you use spells to get where you're at."

That made Javan laugh. "Zulman told me the same thing when I was in the victualing office talking Pripessa into letting me buy straight from her."

"*Zulman* say that?" Siilo asked in dismay. Javan nodded—it was nothing but the truth. Siilo's lip curled. He had a low opinion of everyone who ran the dining cars. The higher anyone's place in the hierarchy, the lower Siilo's opinion. His opinion of Zulman, then, was very low indeed. After a moment, though, he brightened. "Must be so, eh, if even a dingleberry like that can see it?"

"But it wasn't in Dongorland. We're on the way there now. It was back in Liho," Javan reminded him. "And the only thing I know about magic is, I don't know anything about magic."

"That what you say," Siilo said. "Me, I don't know much about magic, neither, but I know sometimes it slop over from where it usually work. Not often, maybe, but sometimes."

Javan remembered the old-time photographs of the dragons pulling The Train into Pingaspor. He'd thought about them the first time he saw dragons replacing the locomotive in Dongorland, but hardly at all since. Magic *could* get out where you didn't expect it to, just as the mechanical arts *could* work well in a place like Marmorica, where you wouldn't expect them to, either (unless you were Bordric, that is). They *could*, but they very seldom did.

"I take it back," Javan said. "I know one other thing about magic after all. If it does slop over, it's never slopped over on me. I'm no wizard, and I don't want to be one."

"It could be." By the way Siilo said that, he didn't believe a word of it. He even explained why, something he didn't always do: "A wizard who boast about what a big wizard he is, he not really much of a wizard. Am I right or am I right?"

"You're right, Siilo. Aren't you always?" Javan answered. Siilo nodded; if he wasn't always right, he wasn't about to admit it, even to himself. By his way of thinking, though, a man could never show he *wasn't* a wizard. If he did well, he had magic working for him. If he did not so well, he was disguising his magic so no one would suspect him. He couldn't win.

Then Siilo said, "You start out in third class with enough to get on The Train and no more, same like me. You gonna end up in first class, sleep on silk, eat till you too wide to go down third-class aisle. You don't call that magic, what you do call it?"

"I call it crap!" Javan ran a hand down his torso. He'd boarded The Train skinny, and skinny he remained. He was sure he would stay skinny forever. Skinny people always are.

Siilo certainly stayed skinny. The old man's shoulders seemed hardly wider than one of the rails down which The Train ran. "All right, maybe you don't get so real fat," he allowed. "But what about the rest?"

"I told you what about it—it's crap," Javan replied. "Luisa and I have to figure out how to buy a second-class ticket for Irini when she gets big enough to need one. Even if we scrape up enough for that, we won't have much left over. First class? You've got to be kidding!"

"You find a way. You do it. People like you, they do it. You still a baby your own self, same like your Irini. By the time you old like me" —Siilo plucked at the long white hairs sticking out of his chin— "you pile up more silver than you know what to do with. You bet you do."

Javan made what he fondly imagined to be a magical pass. Nothing happened afterwards, of course, not least because he didn't believe anything would. "You call me a wizard, and here you make like a soothsayer yourself."

"Fine. Don't listen to me. But don't forget, neither. By the time you find out I'm right, I be way too dead to go, 'Ha! I tell you so!'"

The Train lost its schedule before it got to the city of Dongor. By the way folk used to the mechanical arts thought, it was nobody's fault, nothing like the war between Pingaspor and Namila. A big earthquake had bent and twisted a length of The Railroad into impassability.

Folk used to the mechanical arts talked learnedly about plate tectonics. They talked about fault lines, and slip-strikes, and P-waves and S-waves. They built as well as they could, so the inevitable earthquakes that did come would hurt them less.

In Dongorland, people didn't see things that way. Oh, they built as well as they could, too. But to them, quakes were fights—maybe even wars—between different groups of stone elementals dwelling deep underground. When Dongorians spoke of the living rock, they meant it in ways more literal than those of folk in the rest of the world.

In Pingaspor, savants charted faults and measured crustal stresses. In Dongorland, wizards used different instruments (crystal balls?—Javan had no idea) to get a picture of how the stone elementals' battles fared. And what they could foretell from what they sensed was about as accurate as the information the Pingasporean earth savants gleaned from their seismographs.

Little quakes kept rattling The Train while it waited for repairs to be finished. The salamanders in the snack-sellers' grills no longer smiled; all that shaking made them nervous. It made Javan nervous, too. If you were a human being (or, as the salamanders proved, even if you weren't), how could it do anything else?

But the local wizards said one side in the subterranean war had won such a smashing victory over the other that there wouldn't be any more major battles for a while—only skirmishes. The repairs went on. So did the aftershocks—the victory had been smashing up on top of the ground, too. Javan stayed nervous, but he didn't get hurt.

Passengers didn't get hungry here as they had in the middle of the war zone, though. The Railroad could haul supplies up from behind The Train in a way it hadn't been able to there. It brought carcasses for the dragons (yes, this was Dongorland), food for the dining cars, and, to Javan's delight, a separate shipment for the snack-sellers.

When Zulman found out about that, he ground his teeth again, which only delighted Javan more. And with the shipment to the snack-sellers came a note.

It was written in Pingasporean. That delighted Javan one more time. *I am following how things are going on The Train*, it read. *By all reports, you are doing as well as I could have hoped, or even better. I have found someone from your city to write this for me and let you know I still have my eye on you.* The signature was not in a script Javan could read. If it didn't say *Pripessa*, though, he would have been mightily amazed.

At last, with the bent and ruined rails replaced and the roadbed repaired, the dragons could draw The Train forward toward the city of Dongor once more. The enormous beasts seemed glad to pull. They'd had plenty to eat while The Train waited for The Railroad to get back into working order, but they weren't the sort of creatures that enjoyed staying in any one place for a long time.

There was another brief delay not far in front of the city. The quake had knocked down a bridge. The river spirits and the earth elementals who had supported the piers squabbled over which group of them had the right to uphold the repaired span.

Eventually, with the help of wizards from the city, they reached some kind of compromise. Javan never did find out all the details. But those details were nothing he desperately needed to know. All he needed to know was when The Train could proceed, and how much he had to get for the snack-sellers until that time came.

Some of the buildings in the suburbs of Dongor had fallen down, and some in the city itself. And frightened salamanders, knocked out of their stoves and heaters by the force of the stone elementals fighting far below them, started fires that might have done more damage than the earthquake itself.

A brick wall at the depot had collapsed in the quake. Convicts in glowing orange tunics worked with shovels and hods to clear away the rubble. The tunics literally glowed: some sorcerous effect, no doubt. The Train reached the depot a little after sundown, and the orange light the clothing shed lent its color to the platform. No one wearing anything like that could escape—not for long, anyhow.

The convicts with the hods lugged the broken brickwork over to large, plain carpets floating at the edge of the platform. They dumped the bricks onto the carpets and went back for more, moving as slowly as their guards would let them.

Javan smiled, recognizing that shabby work rate. He hadn't busted his tail when he was working on The Railroad, either. He hadn't even been a convict then, just a kid putting in his time on the corvée. But it wasn't as if he'd been working for himself. He'd been out there because he had no other choice, and he'd performed like it.

His smile quickly slipped. Now he worked hard all the time. He got the rewards for that, but he needed them, too. If he didn't work hard, he wouldn't eat much. He'd wear old, worn-out clothes. He and Luisa wouldn't enjoy their soft second-class seats (and enjoy his he did). They'd never be able to afford that second-class ticket for Irini.

Luisa was starting to think out loud about having another baby. *Two* more second-class tickets? Javan wasn't sure they'd be able to afford those no matter how hard he worked. But he wasn't sure they wouldn't be able to, either. He'd already managed more than he'd ever dreamt he could when he boarded The Train.

He'd also managed more than Siilo had dreamt he could. That made him stand very straight and puff out his chest as far as it would go. His own father was back in Pingaspor. Javan didn't often think about him; he was busy leading his own life here. But Siilo filled some of the place his father had held in his home city.

When a carpet was filled with bricks and mortar and whatever other rubbish the convicts brought, a wizard would make passes—passes he believed in—and guide it down the alleyway toward wherever it would eventually dump its cargo. The convicts' orange tunics cast a sinister, almost demonic, light on the wizards' features. Beneath that glow, though, the wizards looked about as excited as Bordric did while he was grilling sausages.

Javan thought that was a shame. Here these fellows were, doing things that would have been reckoned nearly miraculous in Pingaspor. But they did these things every day. They might as well have been leading ox carts or driving trucks.

And chances were they couldn't grill up even a halfway decent plate of sausages. Who didn't have a special set of talents, whether you called them magic or not?

More passengers than usual boarded at the Dongor depot. Javan wondered whether they were planning to settle in some place where the mechanical arts held sway. If they hoped such places were immune to disaster, they would end up disappointed.

Or perhaps they simply wanted to get on The Train and ride it for as long as their money and their wits held out. That was what Javan had had in mind when he came aboard, as much as he'd had anything in mind at all. You got on. You found some way to keep yourself fed while The Train made its steady way round and round the world. You didn't worry about what would happen farther along The Railroad. When it happened, whatever it turned out to be, you found some way to deal with it. And you went on riding till the next *it* came along.

Some people, on The Train and off it, wondered what the point of a ride like that was. Javan was more interested in getting along than in fine points of philosophy. He had no idea what the point to riding The Train was, or whether there was any. Most of the time, he didn't much worry about it, either.

Round and round, round and round. Often, a circuit of the world on The Train seemed pretty much like the one that had come before it or the one that came right after. Often, but not always. Every once in a while, you came back to discover that the city where you'd boarded had lost its collective mind. Or an earthquake knocked everything all out of kilter.

Or you helped your spouse to the first-aid car and, before too long, the midwife put your daughter in your clumsy arms. Yes, *that* circuit would stick in your mind for the rest of your days. Javan wondered if he'd recall the birth of his second child so vividly.

And life went on whether or not you would remember a particular moment, a particular day, fifty years from now. Regardless of whether it stuck in your mind, you had to go through it. No, you had to get on with it. It seemed to go better when you tried to make things happen and didn't just let them happen. Maybe it didn't—how could you know for sure?—but it seemed to.

Here in Dongorland, the people got what answers they had from magic. That had seemed pretty wonderful to Javan the first time he came here. Dealing with the smiling salamander in the grill and the blue-green elemental in the ice chest was different from fiddling with a gas burner or an electrical cooling unit, all right.

But the people of Dongorland, from everything Javan had seen on The Train and out the window, were just that—people. They fell in love and fell out of love. They quarreled. They made up. They did what they could for themselves and for other people they cared about. They had different tools, but they used them for the same reasons and to get the same kinds of things people everywhere else craved.

In fact, if you listened to the folk of this magic land, even the elementals dwelling deep within the underground stone quarreled the same way people did. And here, far above, the people were still busy cleaning up after them.

Javan did his best to explain some of that to Luisa as they were settling down for the night and trying to get Irini to settle down, too. She gave him a peculiar look. "Did you let them put any mushrooms in your supper?" she asked.

People from nonmagical cities said Dongorland mushrooms could fill your head with mystical visions. People from Dongorland didn't say that was true. They didn't go out of their way to deny it, though. And they charged more for mushrooms than growers anywhere else had the nerve to ask.

"No mushrooms," Javan answered. "I got to thinking about things, that's all."

"Well, think about ways to make this baby quit wiggling and go to sleep," Luisa said irritably. She didn't care about what life meant or whether people in Dongorland were fundamentally different from people in Pingaspor or Namila. She cared about getting a good night's sleep, or at least a halfway decent night's sleep.

And most of the time Javan felt the same way. But every so often, if you kept going around and around on The Train, how could you *not* wonder what the point of it was and whether it had any point at all? Javan chuckled softly.

"What's funny?" Luisa asked through Irini's whimpers. Her tone warned that, whatever it was, it had better be good.

"Oh, nothing, not really." Javan reached for his daughter to see if he'd have any better luck quieting her down. How could you expect your moment of wondering about what things meant to coincide with your spouse's? You couldn't, and Javan's and Luisa's didn't.

Eventually—very eventually—Irini did go to sleep, which meant Javan and Luisa got to go to sleep, too. Javan pried his eyelids open the next morning with two small cups of snarlingly strong coffee. It wasn't a morning where tea would turn the trick.

Fueled by the liquid brain cells, Javan took his questions to Siilo. Yes, he knew Siilo wasn't the most introspective man ever born, which was putting it mildly. But he couldn't very well ask his own father, not here halfway around the world. So he tried Siilo instead.

The old man must have been fond of him, too, because he didn't just walk away or laugh in Javan's face. He did say, "Not something I care about much." He was trying to steer Javan away from those shoal-filled waters.

Javan didn't want to be steered away. "Do you *ever* think about these things?" he asked.

"Little bit, maybe." Siilo's face said he didn't care to admit even so much.

"And?" Javan prompted.

"I get on The Train, I'm a kid, younger than you when you board, like I tell you before," Siilo said, his weathered features softening as he stared back across the years. "I want to get out of my home city bad, bad, bad. So bad I lift this and that to help me make my fare, you know? They yell 'All aboard!' and I jump on! You bet I do! So my city want me gone, too, or else they want me *back*." His laugh held little mirth. "They not find out I lift stuff before I go. Then they forget about me, I hope."

"And?" Javan said again.

"And I still riding, all these years later." Siilo sounded proud of himself, and why not? "I get to be snack-seller's help-er, same way like you. Then I do my own selling, not work for nobody else no more. I get along. But I not sharp operator like you, get whole bunch of people working for me."

"Feh!" Javan still didn't want to think of it that way. "What about the other things, the things that don't have to do with work?"

"What about 'em? Not much time for 'em," Siilo said. "I have friends. I have lady friends, too, sometimes. Not like you and Luisa—no brats I know about. But when I young, pretty girls like me fine, oh, yes. Even now...It can happen, a pretty girl feel sorry for me and my white whiskers and my wrinkles, want to make old man feel good a little while. And you know what?"

Javan took his cue: "What?"

"*Does* still feel good, even once you get old," Siilo said. "Nothing better, for sure. So I keep going. Why not? Sooner or later, they plant me at Liho or Thargorond or some place like that. Or they chuck my carcass into ocean from way up high. Or they cut me in cubes and grill me for snacks. Who knows? Who cares?"

"They won't grill you. You're too tough and stringy," Javan told him.

"Could be. But you never can tell. Maybe I cook up nice. You see pigs like that sometimes." Siilo scrunched up his face and gave an alarmingly convincing grunt. Then he went on, "But even after I gone, somebody like you show how to make super extra delicious snacks, he spice them the way I do, the way I learn you. I get remembered a little bit. How much more you can hope for than you get remembered a little bit after you gone?"

"I don't know," Javan said slowly. Sure enough, you got on The Train when they yelled *All aboard!* You rode as long as you could. You saw what you saw. You did what you did. If you were lucky, they remembered you—a little after you were gone.

Was there anything more to it than that? One more thing Javan didn't know. He might find out. If he did, he hoped he wouldn't for a long time. When he did—if he did—he guessed it would be too late to do him any good. But he wasn't what you'd call sure about that, either.

"Too much waste time," Siilo said. "Back to work!"

"Back to work," Javan agreed.

Introducing
Rachel Turtledove
Harry Turtledove

LIKE HER TWO SISTERS, RACHEL grew up in a house where both her parents were writers. Most of what I write is science fiction and fantasy; so is a good part of what Laura does. It's not surprising, then, that Rachel went to her first sf convention (a Loscon) when she was six months old.

It's also not surprising that—again, like her sisters—she grew up to be a good writer herself. Genetics? Environment? Some of both, probably. I have a first cousin who was a published author and an uncle who was a technical writer, while Laura's younger brother has also sold several fantasy novels and short stories. And the girls all grew up in a house where the printed word was taken seriously. "Books are your friends," we told them, and they believed us.

Reading L. Sprague de Camp's *Lest Darkness Fall* got me interested in Byzantine history and changed my life. Reading Peter Beagle's *The Folk of the Air* turned Rachel toward Japanese history and culture the same way. Writers are dangerous people. They can turn your life around, and you don't even realize till afterwards that they've done it.

Rachel went to the University of California, Riverside, focusing on Japanese history and literature. She studied abroad in Kyoto for several months, and traveled to Tokyo and Hiroshima. After she returned to UCR, she earned her bachelor's degree, covering herself in academic glory (yes, I'm her father, so I get to brag).

About a month after she got to UC Riverside, she noticed a fellow who was in her dorm. And Jason noticed her, too. They clicked, quietly and firmly, and they've been together for the last seven years, and married for three of them now. As someone who was lucky enough to have this happen to him, I know how precious it is.

They live in Northern California these days, in the East Bay. Rachel takes after her mother (who, as well as being a writer, is also an elementary-school librarian) in being patient and understanding and really good with kids. She's teaching preschool and having a terrific time.

When Arc Manor/Phoenix Pick asked me to pick a younger author to work with me, I asked all three of my daughters if they wanted to do that. Rachel was the one who had the interest and the time to take a shot at it. She was up very late meeting her deadline, but she did it. "First Passage," then, is her first published story. I doubt very much it will be her last one, and I don't think that's just a father's pride talking.

ON THE TRAIN

Book Two
FIRST PASSAGE

RACHEL TURTLEDOVE

THE RAILROAD RAN BEHIND ELI'S BACKYARD, but The Train never stopped. The closest station was a week's worth of travel by coach, half a month's journey by foot. Eli had never taken The Train, but she knew its Road quite well.

In a bed of gravel, two lines lay next to each other. East and west to travel the world. The rows of wooden ties stretched on and on in both directions, each one laid just a footstep apart from the next. At night, Eli would climb the ridge behind her parents' old house and walk along the track from one beam to the next. White and gray, the gravel shone like broken bits of moon at her feet. She knew which of the planks were old and soft, where the wood had begun to feel like rot, yet not crumbly enough to warrant replacing. Workers delivered new beams as needed, but even those quickly developed their own sense of softness. Moss dressed the wood, spreading out of knots and grooves in a lacy patchwork. In the moist air, it would keep growing forever, if not for the passage of The Trains.

When a Train passed, it ripped along the ground. It would begin as a tremble in the distance, quickly moving closer, faster and faster. In real towns, ones closer to the stations, Eli knew that The Trains kept to a firm schedule. But out here, those arrivals and departures were a mystery. There was barely enough time for people to scramble out of their houses. Neighbors in Ugara lived too far apart to shout the news to one another, but the rumbling earth was a simple enough way to broadcast an approach. People would drop what they were doing and run toward the base of the embankment that carried the tracks. Staring up at The Train, they would point and shout out, trying to remember details to boast about to friends unfortunate enough to miss out on the rare sight.

The best Trains were the few that passed by at night, during one of Eli's walks. Most folks were asleep in their beds, often too tired to untangle themselves from their mosquito netting and run out into the humid dark. Most nights, nothing came. There could be weeks or even months of nothing but walks with empty tracks. But if she was lucky, Eli would begin to feel a quiver in the air quite unlike wind. Then, a whistle would sound.

Sometimes the whistles were deep, long hoots unfolding through the stillness; sometimes, a series of single-noted shrieks blasted out. Sometimes, it was merely the clanging of a bell. Sometimes, it was a mournful wail, wavering in tones—short, then long again—as if several horns were being sounded at once. With each note, Eli's breath would jam up in her chest, her body tense with listening.

She always had plenty of time to get off the tracks before The Train came.

Settling herself on a tree stump or in a patch of dewy grass, she would watch as it thundered by. The Trains looked different at night. Oh sure, they always looked different. It seemed as if no one in Ugara had ever seen the same train twice. People said that all along the Railroad, too. But at night! Trains turned into long, snaky black bodies, streaming down the tracks, almost impossible to see where one car ended and another car began, except for the lights. Each Train had different lights to guide its way. One might have three yellow beams mounted from its engine. Another had strange blue lanterns, with glowing dots of light inside them that swirled and shimmered, possibly magic! Eli remembered one in particular with narrow red headlights, racing toward her out of the black like demon eyes. Part of her wondered if they *had* been eyes. And a few times, she was able to catch a glimpse of bright rooms inside The Trains and wondered what it would be like to ride herself.

In a week's time, it would finally be her turn.

It was silly to waste the night coming up here. She had told Baroness Vasri she needed to return home to pick up a few things for the journey and say goodbye to her parents. It had been easy enough to fill her rucksack with extra clothes and bathing supplies. As usual, Mother tried to weigh her down further with food—flatbread wrapped in foil paper and small tins of sauces, mint and coconut, to remind her of home. Eli had protested, "The Baroness told me I didn't need to bring anything to eat," but her mother dismissed that with a cluck of her tongue.

"Who knows what foods they make on The Train? No one here," her mother chided. "Maybe it make you sick. Maybe it make you shit for days. Who will look after the children then? You think their mother will change nappies on The Train?"

That had made them both laugh, just picturing the Baroness changing a nappy. Eli grinned just remembering it.

But the real reason she had come back was to climb the ridge once again and look at the Railroad. It stretched out before her, as always. East and west to travel the world. To be sure, she would only be going a little ways, but it would be farther than she had ever gone before. Would the Railroad look different after she had traveled on it? Would she look different?

She sat down, shivering even though it wasn't cold. She sat through the night, but, as usual, no Trains came. It didn't matter; hers was out there, somewhere up that line.

In the morning, she rejoined the Baroness' family. Slowly, they began heading east.

Eli had been so anticipating her first passage on The Train, that she hadn't prepared herself for the grueling carriage ride to the station—trapped in a cab with the Baroness' two small children.

As usual, four-year-old Rinatta and three-year-old Willin were left in her charge. The Baroness followed in the carriage behind with Sela, her personal servant. Willin, only recently three, had entered into his own stage of obsession over The Train, and was ecstatic at the chance to ride. Any enthusiasm Rinatta held for their journey was deeply hidden by her scorn for anything her baby brother loved.

Looking at the tiny carved train Willin clutched in his hand at all times, she sneered, "Trains are for babies."

Willin, determined not to be babyish in any way, protested, "No, they're not."

"Oh, yes they are!"

"No! They're not!"

"Yes! They! Are!"

"Nu-uh!"

"Uh-huh!"

And once started, the back-and-forth battle quickly reduced to barbaric grunting and hair pulling. Eli did her best to sort them out.

"Rinatta, stop teasing your brother. Willin, let go of her braid." Eli helped pry his fingers off one of his sister's strips of dark hair.

Rinatta, her hair now freed, tossed her braids and could not resist whispering one last quip. "You *are* a baby. You're not even toilet-trained."

"Enough!" Eli thundered before hell broke loose again. "Willin is learning just fine for his age. And don't forget you still wear a bed-time nappy, Rinatta."

It was certainly faster to change his wet nappies than having to stop every few hours for Rinatta to take care of business on the side of the road. She needed to go but didn't appreciate the outdoors as a place to do it, and whined endlessly. Eli looked forward to getting to The Train, where the Baroness had promised there would be whole cars converted into washrooms.

Traveling for a week and mostly having to sleep sitting up did not agree with Eli. The novelty also wore off for the children, and they became fussy and bored. At least on The Train Eli hoped she would be able to take them to stretch their legs and explore. In the carriage, she could entertain them with singing songs and clapping games for only so long. She wondered how the Baroness and Sela were passing the time, but she rarely saw them, even when they stopped at night to make camp.

The Baroness was a strange woman. Eli had decided that shortly after entering her service, and nothing came along to change her mind. It wasn't only that she had no interest in her children. Eli assumed that was normal for a woman so busy and so rich, who had moved into a nothing-town like Ugara. Yet she had waited late into her life to have Rinatta, followed quickly by the birth of Willin. Eli knew from her mother, one of Ugara's chief midwives, that a pregnancy at that age often took careful planning. So part of her must have decided she wanted them after all?

The townsfolk had whispered and wondered about the Baroness ever since she moved onto one of the plantations. No one knew anything about the late Baron—if there had even been one. Neither the Baroness nor baby Rinatta had arrived wearing the white robes of mourning. Willin came along a few months later. Eli figured that stuff wasn't her business anyway. The kids were there, so she would take care of them.

"Are we there yet?" groaned Rinatta, pulling Eli from her thoughts. She had to give the child credit. For all their days of travel, she had heard that question only a few times.

Suppressing a smile, she said, "Why don't you look out the window and tell me what you see?"

Rinatta crawled across the seat to roll up the leather window covering. She stuck her head out of the opening and then let out a wild shriek.

"I can see it! The station's just ahead!"

Willin bounced up and down on his bench. "Station! Station's here!"

Eli scooted over quickly to put a firm hand around Rinatta's waist. The child was leaning so far out now, Eli was afraid she might go tumbling into the dirt below.

"I can't see!" wailed Willin.

Without being prompted, Rinatta made room for her brother. Apparently, her excitement over their arrival made her forget to be snotty.

Willin looked out, but the mules must have been kicking up too much dust for he quickly sat back down, rubbing his eyes. "No Train," he reported.

Eli gave him a hug. "It'll come soon. And it won't leave without us!"

She took a peek out the window as well. The jungle had been cleared, leaving the earth bare and red. There was a bend in the road ahead, and coming up on their left was the station. There was a town just behind it. Sao Lindros, that's what it was called. All her life, Eli had seen it as a dot on a map—the closest connection to the real world, yet so unreachable. And here she was. She noticed buildings of all different sizes, all made out of dark, red-brown bricks. *Clay*, thought Eli. *That's why the dirt is red here.* Most of the buildings had thatched roofs, like in Ugara, but Sao Lindros roofs were mostly dome shaped, instead of rising to a point. Beyond that, she could see the station platform! And beside it, the Railroad, always the Railroad.

As they drew up in front, Eli could see people standing under covered awnings, already waiting for The Train to come. Some were leaning against pillars, fanning themselves and trying to keep in the shade. Piles of bags and luggage huddled together in little groups, like bunches of colorful mushrooms. How long had these people been there? Eli wondered how much longer they would have to wait for The Train.

Fortunately, she did not have to hold on to this worry for long. It took her a moment to realize that the coach had stopped. Yet she still felt a strange swaying sensation, as if her body were still moving. Then a familiar quiver began to pass through her.

Eli flung open the door to the cab and kicked the stepladder to the ground. Leaping out, she turned to see her Train.

***

This Train was black with a red underbelly. Even the huge wheels and gears that rushed beneath it were red. Two big lamps were positioned on either side of the engine, sending crisscrossing beams of light onto the track. Gusts of white clouds poured out of its smokestack and streamed over the tops of the passenger cars that followed. Windows flashed by, suddenly replaced by large boxcars and freight containers. The sides of these cars were plastered with posters, still too far off to examine properly.

The whistle shrilled at an almost ear-splitting pitch. Some of the folks gathered on the platform covered their ears, but to Eli it was a welcome cry. She loved the intensity of this salutation and would not have wanted it any other way. Yes, this was her Train!

"That our Train?" Willin's voice came from behind her.

Wrenching her eyes off the great locomotive, Eli saw the children standing up in the carriage. She held out her hand to help them clamber down.

"'Course it's our Train!" Rinatta was scoffing. "There's only one Train in the world. It just goes around and around." She hesitated, then looked up for confirmation. "Right, Eli? One Train."

"I don't know the answer to that," she replied honestly. "I've been watching The Train come down the Railroad for all sixteen years of my life. And I've heard enough different stories and ideas about it to fill each of those years. Some folks'd tell me that there's just one Train, but it can change itself around, like a snake that sheds its skin. Others say, they all look different, so they all must be different. If you wait long enough, you'll see an old Train pass through again. But I don't think anyone in Ugara is old enough to have seen that happen yet."

"It's magic," Rinatta explained loftily to her brother.

"Well, I don't know about that either. There's a few folks in Ugara who can use little bits of magic. Mostly midwives and the healing woman. Out on the Railroad, there should be lots of parts that make much more magic than we do. Where people use it every day, for everything! But I've also heard there's parts that make none at all. So I don't see how The Train could still run there, if it's all magic. Some parts of it must take real work."

Both children nodded. The mystery of The Train (or Trains) was easily accepted by the young. They could appreciate the wonder, rather than trying to pick it apart. Eli felt relieved. If she thought too much on it herself, her head might burst. Or, worse, she might wake up back in her hammock bed in Ugara.

But no, this wasn't a dream. It was real. The Train's wheels and gears groaned and squealed as it pulled into the station in front of them.

"Quickly, children, we must get our things."

The Baroness Vasri climbed out of her carriage and began unwrapping the fastenings that secured their luggage in back. Terhan, the mule driver, hovered next to her, but she made no room to accept any help. Her sleeveless shirt showed off her long, muscular arms, which lifted the two heavy cases with ease.

Eli let Terhan unload the smaller bags from their carriage. She herded the children over and helped both to slip the straps of a small rucksack over their shoulders. Hoisting her own onto her back, she then maneuvered a wheeled case with a handle in front of her.

Sela, the Baroness' servant, emerged at last from the other carriage. She surveyed the scene with her narrow, dark eyes, and gave Eli a curt nod of satisfaction. She did not offer to carry any of their belongings herself, nor did the Baroness ask her to. Sela was far too small and frail, her gray hair pinched up into a bun at the back of her head. When she stood next to the Baroness, they made a strange pairing. The Baroness was extremely tall for a woman, yet her body was thick and stocky, with almost no neck at all. What Sela lacked in height, she did not make up for in girth either—she was straight and bony as a dried stalk of sugarcane. Yet she had served the

Baroness for decades and was closer to her than any other member of their household.

"This way," ordered the Baroness, already striding toward the station.

"You may return home now. We won't be needing any more assistance." Sela murmured to their drivers. Terhan and his brother nodded and returned to their mules, automatically accepting the order.

The group made their way toward the platform, the children darting ahead and then coming back to check on the three shuffling women. Little clouds of red dust puffed out from the wheels of Eli's luggage.

A small hut had been constructed directly in front. The man leaning out its large window grinned toothily at them. "You folks needing some tickets?"

The smile faded as his eyes drifted back and forth between the Baroness and Sela's expressionless faces. After that, he did not even look at Eli or the children.

"We require five first-class tickets," said the Baroness.

"You can pay?" The man's mouth fell open in shock. It was enough that anyone should be able to afford a first-class ticket, let alone five. Eli doubted the ticket-seller could even afford a ride in third-class—if he had ever set foot on The Train at all. His world probably ended here, at the edge of the platform.

"I trust this should suffice." The Baroness unbuckled her case and drew out several canvas pouches, wrapped with gold twine. She untied one and poured some of its contents into her palm.

Small crystals spilled out, catching white, pink, orange shimmers in the sun. Eagerly, the man extended his hand and the Baroness allowed him to pick one up. He turned over its rough edges, admiring its size, then held it up to his lips and gave it a tentative flick with his tongue. His look of surprise changed to one of awe. Eli knew it must be good—she had never seen salt crystals so pure.

"Those will be just fine, ma'am," he stuttered as she passed him the bags. From the back of his hut, he pulled out a sheet of printed paper. He folded it along several creases and punched out five sets of tickets. The Baroness accepted hers, then stepped aside for Sela and Eli to take their own. The man looked uncertainly at the children, and then passed their tickets out as well. "Just head straight through the gate. Only passengers go on from there," he said.

Eli intercepted the children's tickets, but let them take a good look before she put them away. "I'll hold them until we get on board," she told Willin and Rinatta. "We can't lose these. They're too important."

"What does it say?" demanded Rinatta, screwing up her eyes as she stared at all the letters that covered both sides of the ticket.

Eli looked down and found she was not sure. The typed print was small and squiggly, and completely unfamiliar. What's more, the scripts seemed to change. Every few lines looked different; some marks were long with lots of loops, others were short mixed in with flicks and dashes.

Suddenly, Sela spoke. "First Class Ticket. Carriage 6. Compartment 15. Seat 3. Your seat numbers will be different, of course."

"How come it's all funny-like?" asked Rinatta. She certainly couldn't read yet, but at least she knew most of her alphabet.

"Ugaran is not used on the Railroad. It is a nothing tongue, used in a nothing place. Sao Lindros is not much better, but at least you can move away from here."

Rinatta took this in solemnly. "So nobody's gonna know what we say?" she asked.

"Everyone on The Train uses the same words. They come from all over and speak from all over, so there had to be one way to communicate with each other. Like this. When you meet someone new on The Train, you will say 'Kei kei' and give a little bow. That means 'hello.'"

"Kei kei," Rinatta echoed, copying Sela's bob of the head.

Eli was sure her face must look as shocked as the ticket-seller's had when asked for five tickets. She would never have guessed Sela knew so much about the Railroad.

The Baroness did not seem surprised, but she was clearly growing impatient. "Enough, Sela. You can teach them Traintalk later."

Traintalk? What is Traintalk and when did Sela learn about it? wondered Eli as the Baroness hustled them along through a turnstile gate. Its metal bars shifted as each of them passed through.

"All aboard! All aboard, Sao Lindros!" someone was calling.

Yellow arrows marked the way to The Train. The other passengers were already lining up, showing their tickets to a conductor in a blue uniform with a high collar. There weren't too many people, most of them much older than Eli. She noticed a tired-looking man with dark skin and a thick beard, two women wearing colorful wraps. What had brought them to The Train? How far could they travel?

Another conductor noticed their party and hurried over. "First-class?" he asked in a halting voice. Eli realized he was not speaking Ugaran, but she could still understand him. Evidently in Sao Lindros they spoke something still pretty close to her own words, not different enough to be called a separate language. She wasn't completely out of her element yet. She could see his hair, damp with sweat under his blue cap. His jacket and long pants were much too heavy to be wearing under the beating sun.

"You don't need to wait in line, ma'am," he told the Baroness.

He ushered them toward the front of The Train. At least Eli could recognize numbers printed on the sides of the cars. Nine, eight, seven, six!

The black doors were already open. A portable step had been secured to the platform to let them climb in.

Willin grabbed at her hand and squealed in delight. "We're here!" He and Rinatta looked ready to tear inside and own the place.

"Hold on, hold on, let me get in first." Eli fumbled with her wheeled luggage, not looking forward to lugging it up the steep steps. A ramp would have been far more convenient. Why couldn't they have had that?

Someone tapped her on the shoulder.

Eli jumped. A gangly young man, close to her own age, stood beside her, even though she had not noticed his approach. He was dressed in all black, except for his tan ankle boots which were made out of a soft-looking leather. His hair was a sandy brown, tied back in a short ponytail. He grinned at her and said something she could not understand.

Still feeling startled, Eli shook her head at him.

He repeated his words to her. They had a clipped and easy sound to them, but she couldn't follow. Then he gestured to her bag and pointed to himself. He held out his hand expectantly.

"The boy wants to help us with our luggage," Sela translated.

"No one touches our things," the Baroness snapped, glaring at him. "Bou." Clearly, that meant "no."

The young man shrugged his shoulders and tossed the Baroness a placating smile as he backed off. He sidled further down the platform and out of sight.

"You didn't have to run him off," sighed Sela. She was the only one who dared speak so straight to the Baroness. "He was probably just looking for money."

"It makes no difference," said the Baroness. She hoisted her own bags up without great difficulty.

"I'll keep an eye on the children for a moment, Eli. You get the rest of the things up," Sela offered.

"Thanks," muttered Eli. She tugged her luggage up one step at a time and entered The Train.

The floor was carpeted, thick and green, reminding Eli of the moss that grew over the Railroad ties back home. The wheels of her bag sank into it. Awkwardly, she followed the

Baroness down a long aisle, shame-faced at how her bag dragged uncooperatively with each step.

The Train was even grander than she could have imagined. Glossy wooden paneling alternated with glass windows that led into individual train compartments. Inside, Eli glimpsed huge plush chairs, upholstered in the same green as the carpet. Other passengers were turning their heads to look at the new arrivals. Eli ducked her head down and kept her eyes on the floor. She realized her wheels were leaving little track marks in the carpet. Behind her, she could hear Willin and Rinatta creating their own scene, gleefully exclaiming over everything they passed.

The Baroness stopped. "Here. Compartment fifteen. Eli, this is for you and the children. Sela and I will be across from you in number seventeen. Please get them settled in. You shall remain here until the dinner meal is served. I will return to bring you to the dining car."

Of course. The Baroness would not let herself be trapped in a confined space with her son and daughter for any great length of time. And they would be on The Train far longer than any carriage ride. It would be up to Eli to keep them occupied. The Baroness did not wait to see them in; she disappeared into the opposite compartment without offering further instructions.

Eli noticed her compartment door had shiny gold handles, shaped like flower blossoms. Cautiously, she turned the knob.

Everyone inside turned to look at her.

The compartment was small, but already held three other occupants. A man and a woman were seated comfortably together on the side with an empty seat. Eli saw that they were a couple. They both shared the same plumpness and rosy cheeks. The woman's ash-blonde hair was streaked with silver threads; although the man was mostly bald, his beard was graying in uneven patches. The other side of the car had three seats, all of which were taken by a stern-looking man with a hooked nose. He sat with his back against the window, his long legs stretched across the other two seats. As Eli entered, the man tucked up his legs, almost suppressing a horrified look as Willin and Rinatta both poked their heads in behind her. Eli did not blame him—surely no one would appreciate having a Train ride interrupted by the presence of these two rambunctious little ones.

At that moment Rinatta let out a moan. "We don't have to stay here, do we? I don't *like* it!"

"Rinatta, stop! You're being rude!" Eli hissed, flushing.

Fortunately, none of the companions seemed to understand. In fact, the plump woman actually began to smile. She spoke in what Eli was beginning to recognize as the clickety-clack sound of that Traintalk again.

Eli shook her head to show she didn't speak Traintalk. The woman raised her eyebrows, then got to her feet. She gave Eli a comforting pat on the shoulder and then pointed to the wall above the seats. An enormous brass rack was secured to it for storing luggage. Underneath the thick bars, Eli saw numbers printed above each headrest.

"Oh!" She took out their tickets and looked for the numbers. At least she could recognize those. They needed seats one, two, and three. The stern man was sitting in seat number one. "Um—" Eli hesitated, unsure of what to do.

The woman quickly realized her dilemma. She turned to the man and pointed at their tickets, speaking rapidly.

"Sim." The man was nodding resignedly. He moved to the opposite side of their compartment, filling up the rest of the row. Eli realized he had simply been taking advantage of the empty seats and giving the couple more space as well. Now every spot was taken.

"I'll sit in the middle and you two can take turns in the seat next to the window," Eli decided. "Willin, you go first. Hop on up."

She expected Willin to be overjoyed, but instead he burst into tears. "Noooo, Eli. Noooo," he sobbed, tears suddenly pouring down his cheeks. Rinatta, who had been pouting for a few minutes, took one look at her brother's face and abandoned any attempts to keep herself together. "I wanna go home," she wailed, and she started to cry too—loudly, to make sure her sobs could be heard over Willin's.

So much for trying to keep things fun. They were overwhelmed. Eli couldn't be cross with them, even though she dreaded what kind of first impression this double meltdown was making on their new travel companions. She put Rinatta onto a seat and then sat down with Willin on her lap. She wrapped her free arm around Rinatta, who usually pushed away from any type of hug.

"I know it's scary. It's a whole new world. I'm scared, too. It's all right to be a little bit scared at times like this," she reassured them, annoyed at the squeak in her own voice.

Gently patting them on the back, Eli hummed a little soothe-song charm she had learned from her mother. She rarely used it anymore, since it was meant for babies who needed help going to sleep. Fortunately, the children didn't have enough energy to go into full-on hysterics. The song seemed to work, for they both quieted. Willin stopped flailing and let her snuggle him a bit. Rinatta leaned heavily against her.

Someone knocked on their door and then opened it. Another uniformed conductor leaned inside. Unlike the sweating man on the platform, he made no extra effort to be polite, even though everyone here was riding first-class.

Eli could tell he meant business. His face was all points, from nose to chin, with eyes as narrow and savage as a rat.

"Tickets. Tickets," he ordered. That Eli understood. Was he speaking Traintalk?

Slowly, all of them produced their tickets. Eli noticed the couple's tickets looked different from hers, and the hooked nosed man's was different from both. The couple had large papers, folded over many times, while the man had a plastic card. Yet they were all covered in the same variety of writing, lines and lines of different languages.

The conductor unbuckled a long wand from his belt, with a flat metal head. He waved the wand over each ticket and it made a small beep.

The man gave them a tight nod, more like a little jerk of the head. Clearly, all of their tickets passed his inspection, for he reattached the wand to his belt. Without another word, he backed out of their compartment, his head down, so that chin tucked into throat. Eli watched through the aisle window as his hunched body moved on down the aisle. Even with this retreat, Eli felt a strong anxiety among her new companions.

The plump woman took a deep breath and muttered something under her breath. Eli didn't need to know any Traintalk to understand that it was a word unbefitting their refined surroundings. However, it made the men laugh, breaking the tension in the compartment.

From out on the platform, Eli could hear thumps and scrambling feet. All The Train doors were being slammed shut. Someone blew a whistle, a high shriek, and then The Train blasted its own in reply. Mechanical squeals and shifting gears shuddered to life beneath them. With a little tug, The Train began to move. Eli could feel her body gently swaying, rocked by The Train's movement. This was it! They were really going!

Growing up next to the Railroad, she had daydreamed about this moment many times. Excitement began to replace her nervousness. Little details, things her imagination could never have brought to her, leaped out. Her cushioned seat, soft yet strangely dense, seemed to have molded itself under her weight to grant her perfect comfort and support. She rested her chin on the top of Willin's ruffled hair and gazed out the window. The red earth of Sao Lindros flowed steadily past. For an instant, she spotted a woman steadying a huge basin on her head with one hand while swishing a stick at a herd of geese with the other. Then she was gone. The tracks panned away from the center of town, traveling closer to more of the red-brown huts with their domed roofs. People were ducking out onto their back porches, jumping and gesturing at The Train. Eli's eyes blinked past vegetable gardens, rabbit hutches, and rows and rows of laundry, strung up like so many flags waving good-bye to her. Surely these were things she would have seen in Ugara as well. How strange to be finally on the other side.

The Train surged forward, falling into a steady rhythm of speed. Slashes of green began to dot the red ground, first little flecks here and there, but then showing up thicker and deeper as the settlement fell behind and jungle reclaimed the land. Trees rose before Eli's eyes, filling up everything that lay before them and soon covering just as far behind them as she could still see. Unlike on the high ridge, where she had walked so many nights, now The Train made its way deep into the jungle. The arms of the trees bent together above them, weaving into an endless leafy tunnel. Patches of sunlight still broke through, but the outside world seemed dimmer and stranger than ever before.

"When are we going home, Eli?" Rinatta asked quietly, still resting against her.

"Not for a while. I don't know how long it will be exactly." Eli always tried to speak plainly but truthfully with her charges. "Your mama, she's very important and she's got some things to take care of out in the world. That's her own business, not ours. She's just taking us with her, to keep her family close."

"We never even get to see her," muttered Rinatta. "Sela comes round more."

"Well, maybe it'll be different now that we're all on The Train. Or maybe it won't. But no matter what, we've got a lot of new things and places to see and people to meet."

At that, Rinatta looked curiously at the three adults sitting across from them. She did not flinch when she saw them all look directly back at her. Instead, she stuck out her tongue at them, which made the older woman chuckle. The woman seemed surprisingly jovial, definitely more amused than insulted. Eli suspected she'd had children of her own at some point to develop this talent.

"Rinatta, do you remember the words Sela used to say hello?" prompted Eli, trying to rein in the girl's manners.

Despite her attitude problem, Rinatta's mind was quite sharp for her age. "Kei kei," she blurted out, even remembering to bob her head in a little bow.

The other passengers exchanged glances and then each repeated the greeting back to her. Willin, perking up and trying to follow anything his sister did, shyly chanted, "Kei kei, kei kei," more to himself than to the grown-ups.

Now it was Eli's turn. She pointed to herself and said, "Eli," and then touched each child on the head, naming them as well.

The woman was positively beaming by then, her entire face becoming as rosy as her cheeks. "Ahn Pria," she identified herself, then gave her husband an encouraging nudge.

He coughed, making his mustache twitch. "Ahn Uma," he said, confirming that they shared the same family name.

The hooked-nosed man gave Eli a long, curious look before speaking. "Nassan." He wore a beautiful scarf, twisted up around his head, with a long tail of extra fabric hanging down his shoulder. It was dark gray, with thick bands of gold thread woven through it. Eli wasn't sure how old he was. Older than her, but not beyond thirty. She smiled hopefully at him, and he at least didn't frown. She sensed he was still not happy about his Train compartment filling up with children.

But he surprised her. He reached under his seat and lifted out a wicker box. From it, he took out a glass container with a rubbery lid. He popped off the lid, and showed the group its contents: blue, round berries and slices of banana.

He held the fruit out to Eli and the children, holding up one finger, indicating how much they should take. Eli took a banana slice and the children each took a berry, staring at Nassan in great curiosity. Did he consider these special treats? Eli wondered that he should share some of his tiny supply with them, already feeling her heart warm toward his sudden generosity.

Rinatta rolled her berry between her fingers, giving it a close inspection, but Willin immediately went to drop his in his mouth. Quickly, but gently, Nassan reached across and grabbed his hand.

"Bou." He shook his head to indicate "no." Nassan lifted his hands palm up, to show they should wait. Willin froze, his mouth still hanging open, but more curious than scared.

Slowly, Nassan raised his hands to the scarf draped over his shoulder. He moved it to the side and tucked it behind him. Willin gave a yip of delight.

On his shoulder was a lizard. It had red-brown and green scales, with a fanlike crest around its neck. Its eyes were a dark orange.

Knowing what was expected of him now, Willin scooted out of Eli's lap, holding the berry up to the lizard. Eli was again impressed with Nassan's gentleness. He showed Willin how to place the berry in the palm of his hand, stretching his fingers out, tight and flat. The lizard, already smelling food, marched down Nassan's arm and straight up to Willin. The boy was stifling giggles, but did his job proudly. Quick as could be, the lizard's tongue darted out, nabbing the berry and popping it whole in its mouth.

"Ew!" said Rinatta, looking revolted. But her exclamation was immediately followed with another one: "My turn now!" She got in front of her brother and offered up her berry. The lizard gulped it down with ease, leaving Rinatta flailing her hand up and down, delightedly squealing, "Ew! Ew! Ewwww!"

Eli's banana was devoured equally fast, the touch of the tongue like a puff of air. She and the children learned how to say *thank you* in Traintalk.

After its snack, Nassan called the lizard back up to its perch on his shoulder with a tap of his fingers. It settled down, spiraling its tail around his neck.

The Train riders settled down as well, the more experienced passengers glad to get back to the rhythm of their travels. Eli was pleased to see that Nassan's introduction of his pet had worked like magic, making the children forget the strangeness of the new place. They were chattering away to each other, getting along far better than they had in the carriage. Inwardly, Eli rejoiced, hoping they could keep it up.

Suddenly, her ears pricked to a familiar phrase. "I have to poo poo," Willin announced with some urgency.

Eli surged with the sudden adrenaline those words give. "You mean in your nappy? Already?"

"Nu-uh." Willin shook his head. "I have to poo poo now."

"Okay!" Eli assessed the situation. Willin was getting better at recognizing his bodily urges, but it usually took him a while to work through an actual bowel movement. They definitely had a few minutes to locate The Train's nearest washroom. She stood up. "Let's go. Come on, Rinatta, you have to come too."

"But I don't have to go!" the girl complained.

"Well, you can try. If you don't go, you can just wash your hands."

Eli pulled a small bag of toileting supplies and a dry nappy out of her rucksack. She looked hopefully at the plump woman, Pria. Not knowing what else to do, she unsubtly pointed to Willin's bottom.

Pria got the message and pointed that Eli should make a left out of their compartment.

Eli smiled a thank you and they headed out into the aisle.

"Follow me. It must be this way." Eli marched the children along, not letting them take the time to gawk at their surroundings.

The Train moved smoothly, but now that she was standing, Eli found herself wobbling a little—she felt any bumps and sways more. Eventually, she found her Train legs and made her way down.

She had to push open a heavy sliding door and cross through a strange, short hallway with black, unsteady walls like a giant accordion. At the other end was another sliding door, leading into the next car. She made her way down through more first-class compartments, through another accordion-hall, and at last reached the lavatory car, which was divided in half for men and women's use, marked clearly by white silhouettes.

Eli hustled the children toward the women's half. Unfortunately, Rinatta noticed the sign. "Willin's not a *girl*," she said, aghast. "He can't go in there."

Eli gritted her teeth. "Yes, he can. He's with us."

"But—"

"Just come inside. It's for families too, I expect." Eli walked them through the partition that separated the genders.

Then she stopped and stared. Surely The Train was already magic! The room was warm with fresh steam and smelled of lavender. The floor had become pink and white checkered tiles, with a pearly sheen to them, like the inside of the clam shells Eli used to dig out of the Ugaran River. Rows of shiny gold faucets lined one wall, mounted over a long porcelain basin. The opposite side held private stalls, each with its own latrine. In the corner, there was a hinged board attached to the wall, with the symbol of a baby painted on it. The steam came from the far end of the lavatory car, where several stalls were reserved for showering.

Eli had never seen a washroom so grand! To her, the Baroness's tiled outhouse with running water had been something to admire. Now she did not know what to think!

"Gotta go now, Eli." Willin tugged at her shirt in earnest.

"Right." Briskly, Eli took Willin into the closest stall and boosted him onto the seat. He sat, swinging his legs and holding onto the sides. He was really too little for it.

Frowning, Eli stuck her head back out. "Rinatta, you go too," she said.

"But Eli, I don't have to go!"

"I'd think after all our stops by the side of the road, you'd be happy to use a real toilet." Eli reminded her of their less attractive options.

Still grumbling, Rinatta went into the next stall. A few moments later, Eli heard her yank the chain to flush.

"I make pee pee too!" cheered Willin from behind her.

"Good for you!" Eli congratulated him, turning around. "You're getting to be such a big boy—Wait! Willin! You're not done! Sit down, sit down, sit down!"

Too late. Willin had been sitting too far forward on his seat and suddenly a yellow stream came flooding over the edge, instead of going into the basin.

"Is that pee? Willin peed on the floor!" Rinatta bounced out of her own stall and came over to look. "Willin peed on the floor! Ick, what a baby! Baby!"

Willin's face grew red and crumpled in dismay. He shook his finger at his sister, letting out a wordless cry. He fell back on one of his favorite phrases. "Nooo, Eli, nooo!"

"It was an accident. It's all right, Willin. Everybody has accidents," Eli tried to talk over their din, but she didn't reassure him much. "Come on Willin, let's go around the puddle—no, don't step in it. Here, we'll get you wiped up."

Ignoring Rinatta's taunts of "Baby," she cleaned Willin and got a fresh nappy on him. She made sure he was carefully dried and rubbed some of her mother's salve on his bottom—sitting in the carriage for so long had given him a rash. She also had to stash his pants; they'd gotten some trickles of urine on them. What hadn't? She looked around for something to clean the lovely pink tiles.

She wadded up as much of the toilet paper as she dared use to sop up the mess. It still wasn't enough....Should she use one of the embroidered hand towels by the faucets?

Still crouched by the puddle, Eli suddenly heard an exclamation of surprise. Glancing out of the stall, she saw a young woman wrapped in a silken robe. She was frozen, dragging a comb halfway through damp, red hair, having just gotten out of the shower. She was staring at Eli.

"*No, no no!*" Eli understood that Traintalk and clearly so did Willin and Rinatta. The woman continued to jabber, shaking her head and motioning for Eli to get up. She walked over to the corner and rang a bell. It chimed pleasantly.

Eli was still gaping, not sure if she should get up or not, when a woman in a blue uniform rushed into the lavatory with a basket tucked under her arm.

Spotting Eli, she gestured for her to get up. Bewildered, Eli obeyed, and the woman sprinkled a fine blue powder on the floor. Whatever it was, it stopped Willin's pee from spreading any more—it seemed to freeze it into a solid mass. The woman, somehow squatting gracefully despite her uniform's trim skirt, scraped it all up with a tool that looked like a spatula. She then poured it into the toilet, flushing it away. The floor was left spotlessly clean.

"Uh—*thank you!*" Eli remembered to say.

The woman shook her head and babbled at Eli, with several polite bows to the children as well. She was apologizing for not being there sooner to clean up the mess, Eli realized.

Wait! She wanted to be able to say. *This is wrong. You're acting like I'm really first-class. I'm a servant, just like you.*

But she didn't know how. Yet.

The red-haired woman rolled her eyes and went off to finish brushing her hair.

Numb, Eli got the children back to their compartment. She didn't even feel embarrassed about Willin racing down the aisles without any proper pants on besides his nappy. She was out of her league here.

She got them settled into their seats and read some storybooks until they got tired. The light outside had dwindled away.

Somewhere far away, a gong rang. Their companions began to get up.

Pria patted Eli on the knee and pantomimed eating. Clearly, she expected them to accompany the group. Eli was getting hungry, and she knew the children would be soon. But she remembered the Baroness had told her to wait until she returned.

"Go without us. We're coming later," Eli said, waving her arms to show they should leave without them.

Shrugging, Pria, Uma, and Nassan all left.

The compartment was strangely quiet—Rinatta and Willin both dozed. Eli noticed that someone, probably the tall Nassan, had hoisted their largest suitcase up onto the storage rack above their seats. Despite his stern face, Eli suspected he had a hidden sense of nobility.

She wasn't sure when she nodded off herself, but when she woke up, the lights were coming on inside The Train. An amber glow filled the room. Willin and Rinatta were both crashed out. The row opposite them was still empty—their companions still had to be at dinner.

The door to their compartment opened smoothly. At last—here was Sela! The tiny woman chuckled when she saw the sleepy bunch. Even traveling so far in her old age did not faze her—her perfectly tattooed eye makeup and darkened lips always looked fresh.

Sela held out a tray. "The Baroness regrets she wasn't able to make it to the dinner. She decided you should eat here rather than go to the dining car on your own."

Huh. I bet she forgot she said she'd come back for us, thought Eli. From past experience, she knew that as soon as the children were out of her sight, the Baroness Vasri had trouble remembering their existence.

"I bought these from a snack-seller," the old woman continued. "They were a little expensive, but tasty."

Eli nudged the children awake and they devoured the seasoned vegetables and meat, served on bamboo skewers. They were juicy and delicious.

"It's been a long day," Sela said.

"Tell me about it," muttered Eli.

"Well, let's get the children into bed," Sela suggested. "Tomorrow will only be here too soon."

After one more trip to the lavatory—this time without any incidents—Eli followed Sela down to the sleeper car. It was lined with bunk beds, each pair separated by soft, gray curtains for privacy.

Eli got Willin and Rinatta settled into the lower bunk. She knew they were still worn out, since Rinatta barely complained about having to share with her brother, apart from threats to bash his head in if he kicked her or wet the bed from a leaky nappy.

Eli sat next to them until they were both out and then climbed into her own bunk. The mattress was soft as clouds and the blankets equally fluffy. Too tired to even think about the strangeness, the wonderfulness, of it all anymore, Eli went to sleep.

"It's too dark!"

Eli woke to a cry of astonishment and fear.

"It's too *dark*!"

It came again, more desperate now. *Willin*.

Somewhere in the black sleep of The Train, someone giggled. She could hear other rustles from disturbed sleepers and a few titters.

Drawing back her bunk's privacy curtain, Eli was impressed at how much light it blocked out. The aisle outside had a dim light, and the floor was marked with a chain of glowing lights. She climbed out of her bed and crawled into the one below, leaving the curtain partially open to let in some light.

Willin was snuffling and Rinatta had somehow slept through it all. He embraced Eli furiously.

"Eli, it got all black. I looked and I looked and I couldn't find anything. Not even the bed. I couldn't find you," he mumbled against her.

"Sh, shhhh," she whispered. "I should have remembered you like a nightlight in your room. We just won't close the curtain all the way from now on. How does that sound?"

He nodded in response.

"Let's be quiet now. The other passengers are still sleeping. We don't want to wake them up."

He settled down and soon went back to sleep. Luckily, he stayed that way.

But Eli was wide-awake. Despite her luxurious bedding, she could not get comfortable. Her comforter felt too hot, so she kicked it off, and flipped her pillow over. It was refreshing to rest her cheek against the cool side, but it did nothing to bring her closer to sleep. A scared child booted you to full alert.

That and a full bladder.

With both children still fast asleep, Eli decided she might as well get a head start for the day. First a trip to the toilet and then maybe a shower by herself. Rinatta usually woke up a little after sunrise, which couldn't be too far off now.

Slipping softly out of bed again, Eli made her way to the lavatory car. She didn't see any other passengers out of their beds, and the compartments she passed were all empty as well.

Entering the lavatory, she was still impressed with shell-pink floors and glittering faucets—*hang on.*

The faucets were gold before. Yes. They had been gold with two little knobs shaped liked flowers, like The Train's compartment doors. She hadn't spent long admiring them, but after helping the children wash their hands multiple times, she definitely had noticed them.

Now the faucets had long silver necks, with a curve at the top. No flowers or extra adornments—they were very sleek, with no handles at all.

Perplexed, Eli approached the sink. The white porcelain basin was still the same. Had one of the workers come in to replace all the faucets overnight? How strange!

She gently touched the metal with one finger. Nothing happened. What made the water come out?

She touched it again, softly. When that produced no result, gave it a firmer tap. Still nothing. Confused, she waved her hand under the spout.

Suddenly, water rushed out!

Eli pulled her hand back in surprise, then laughed at herself. Clearly, this was a smart faucet! It knew when you needed to wash!

Still amused, she went into the stall. The toilet looked different too. It was shorter, squatter, with a little panel of buttons on the side. This was far too much for any servant to have accomplished, Eli realized. The Train had changed itself. She wasn't sure how, but she knew she was right. People always said The Train changed its appearance from station to station. If it could do that, why not change itself inside as well?

The buttons turned out to be for gentle sprays—one to rinse off with water, the other to dry with warm air. When she stood up, the waste flushed away instantly, on its own. This was like no magic Eli had ever imagined. It was better.

Next, she investigated the shower stalls. Each had a sunken floor and a drain in the middle. Each one also had a little bamboo footstool in the corner and bottles of liquidy soaps secured to the wall. Outside were hooks to hang your clothes and shelves with pristinely folded towels.

Eli undressed and showered. There were two knobs, one for hot water, the other for cold, but she couldn't figure out how to get the right amount of each. She was either scalded or freezing. She rinsed off the fragrant soap as fast as she could and got out.

Wrapping herself with a towel, she dried off and put her nightgown back on. Her regular clothes were still in her luggage. She'd need to go get them, as well as fresh outfits for Rinatta and Willin.

Twisting the towel around her damp hair, she left the lavatory car and made her way down to Compartment Fifteen. Big windows lined the aisles and she could see streaks of orange and pink lining the blue ends of night on the horizon.

She went into the compartment.

A man slept on the chair. In her chair. He was not Nassan or Ahn Uma.

Eli was so surprised, she let out a little shriek before she could stop herself. Embarrassed, she started to clap a hand over her mouth, but then changed her mind and crossed both her arms over her breasts. Her nightgown wasn't revealing, but she'd never been so skimpily dressed when alone with a man before.

He opened his eyes and stared at her, so keenly that she felt she might as well have been naked. His eyes were green and he had messy sandy hair. She recognized him—the young fellow who'd offered to carry their bags into The Train!

A look of recognition also crossed the man's face. Then he grinned at her, a quick, crooked curve of the lips. He was probably around twenty, Eli guessed, but his features were drawn sweetly, eyes almost too close together, still childlike. His expression reminded her of that impish-look Willin put on when he got caught doing something he knew was slightly naughty, but not worth getting into Big Trouble over.

Yes, that was exactly what this man looked like now. Like he was hoping he could weasel out of Big Trouble.

Was he a thief? Did they have thieves in first-class? Frowning, Eli took a quick inventory of the compartment. The luggage and bags were still stowed on their racks, jammed in tightly, so they did not appear to have been rifled. As far as Eli could tell, the man had just been sleeping. Was he a new passenger?

He ducked his head in a little bow, clearly embarrassed. He pointed to the door and started to get up, ready to leave. In this, she saw Rinatta, who tended to vanish for hours after getting busted for some small crime, only returning when she was sure you'd had enough time to forget to be angry with her. Evasive, but often effective.

Unsure of what Train-protocol demanded of her, Eli made room for him to go. With a nod of gratitude, he slid past her. His steps were quick, jungle-cat-like, in his soft, soundless boots. In a few moments, he could be down the aisle and gone from view.

"Wait!" Eli called, raising her hand to show stop. The man turned and hesitated.

"*Name?*" Eli blurted out, one of the few Train-talk words she'd grasped that afternoon.

"Ah!" This time the man's grin spread over his whole face. "Lucca!"

"I'm Eli. Eli." She pointed to herself.

"Eli!" He repeated and bowed formally to her, a deep bend at the waist with an extra sweep of his arm to show her he was making a joke of it. Then he darted off.

Well, she might not understand much about Train-life yet, but that bow told her a lot. Lucca wasn't a first-class passenger, or not a proper one. She didn't think he was somebody's servant, either. He lacked seriousness—he was playful, but in a way that liked to test boundaries. She knew the type—though usually they were two-year-olds.

Still puzzling over their brief encounter, she got down her suitcase and selected clothes for herself and the children.

They were already awake by the time she got back to their bunk. Rinatta had gotten up in the top bunk and was hanging dangerously far over the railing to make faces at her brother.

Willin was giggling like mad, but switched as soon as he spotted Eli. "Stop, stop, make her stop, Eli. She makes faces at me!"

"I think sleeping in a real bed again has made her silly!" Eli grinned, not about to be taken in by his reversal. She grabbed a firm hold of Rinatta and lowered her, still upside down, from the upper. The girl shrieked with laughter as Eli swung her back and forth before flipping her onto the bottom bunk. Willin scrambled out of the way so she didn't squish him.

"Come on, let's get dressed and figure out how they do breakfast in this place," said Eli, handing out shirts and pants.

"They'll be serving it up in the dining car shortly."

Eli looked up and saw Sela standing next to their bed. She appeared to have showered and looked refreshed. Even her fingernails had a new coat of a dark plum-colored polish. She joined them on the mattress and played a little clapping game to occupy Willin while Rinatta got dressed. "Hickory, bickory, bumble bee. Won't you say your name for me?"

"Willin!" squealed the boy on cue.

Everyone was in a good mood as they proceeded to the dining car. Sela led the way to show them where to sit.

The entire car had been converted into a glamorous restaurant. Floor to ceiling, the walls were giant windows, interspersed with coppery-brown panel curtains, to provide shade from bright sunlight. There were a dozen or so round tables, draped with white cloths. Passengers were already taking their seats while the morning meal was served.

From across the room, Pria from their compartment spotted them and began waving for them to come join her.

As they made their way over, Eli noticed that each table was marked with three numbers. Pria's table had little cards in the center that said Fifteen, Sixteen, Seventeen.

"Our compartment numbers," Sela explained. "Every day, we eat with the passengers who ride closest together."

Looking back and forth between them, Pria beamed, her plump cheeks glowing bronze like the sun. Assuming the nature of their conversation, she patted the seat next to her husband for Eli to sit down, exclaiming happily.

"She says we sit together to make better friends." Sela translated crisply. Her lips twitched a little in distaste for the word "friends." Like the Baroness, Sela didn't enjoy social engagements.

And yet, she somehow had picked up plenty of Traintalk! Eli wondered how much she didn't know about the old servant woman. Realizing she was staring, she shook her head and greeted Pria and Uma with polite smiles.

For the children, there were little box seats that could be strapped onto the bottom of the dining chairs for support. This was fortunate, for without it, the table would have been much too high. A servant came around with a platter of fresh fruits and flaky biscuits with jam. The children devoured them with gusto and even Eli thought she had never eaten something so heavenly.

Halfway through, Nassan showed up and joined their table. He still looked sleepy and did not talk much until he had drunk two cups of black coffee. Several other passengers drifted in as well and took their seats at the table. Eli peeked at them, but tried not to attract too much attention to herself and her ignorance of life on The Train.

Some had dressed for breakfast with careful attention, while Eli found herself wondering how others could have afforded a first-class ticket at all. Across from her sat a scruffy-looking man in a purple T-shirt. He had a frizz of brown hair, as if he had been out in a lightning storm. His arms and the back of his neck were covered with the same fuzz, making him a great bear of a man. Two mustached men took seats at the opposite end of the table. They were dressed almost identically and much more formally in buttoned shirts and gray linen jackets. Both had silver badges pinned on their pockets. They seized cups of coffee and fell deep into discussion with Nassan. An elderly woman with a cane clunked her away across the dining carriage and then took a chair at their table as well.

Eventually, only one seat remained empty.

The Baroness.

Eli was sure she hadn't joined this group for dinner last night. Now she was skipping breakfast. The Baroness clearly wanted nothing to do with the other passengers. Did she consider them beneath her? Surely she was not so important as that? None of Eli's tablemates paid much attention to the unfilled spot. Perhaps they were used to a constant flow of changing passengers. The car was filling up, but some scattered seats were left. Eli didn't see any other travelers with children.

Her thoughts were interrupted when Rinatta dropped a biscuit in her lap, jam side down. Eli poured a little water from her glass onto her cloth napkin and told the girl how to mop it up.

A murmur of voices drew her attention to the back to the car. A conductor was stepping up onto a little platform beside the wall. It was a stage, Eli realized, with three large stringed instruments propped next to some stools. But the conductor was not about to begin a performance.

He was the rat-faced man—the ticket checker. The tester.

He drew out a whistle from around his neck and blew a short blast that made her ears ring. Then he held up a long piece of paper: some sort of flyer. It was printed in bold, black ink. At the top was a blocky illustration. Even from so far away, Eli could make it out: a Train compartment with a figure of a person going out through the door. At the bottom were lines and lines of various scripts.

The conductor spoke rapidly, making his announcement or explaining the paper.

"What's he saying?" hissed Rinatta, in her best attempt at a quiet voice.

"Shhhh!" Eli hushed her, pressing her finger over her lips. "Wait."

The conductor continued. No matter how hard she tried, Eli could not make out his message, so she gave up and studied the man instead. He was not an animated speaker. His uniform was wrinkled and there was a stain on his tunic. His skin was ashy, his lips stretched in an ugly grimace. She couldn't tell if it was because he was reporting bad news or out of disgust for this crowd. His figure was hunched, as if he hated to be the focus of their attention, and yet there was defiance in the way he returned their gaze. Yes. Defiance, almost viciousness. His eyes hunted among them. Looking—for what?

Abruptly, he finished his speech. Without waiting for a response from the passengers, he stepped down from the stage and stalked back across the car. He stopped briefly at the entrance, only to pin his poster to the door. Then he was gone. Everyone in the car started to talk at once.

Eli turned to Sela. "What was all that about?"

The servant woman took a sip of water, frowning. "Slinkers."

"What's a slinker?" demanded Rinatta.

"I'm afraid my Traintalk is rusty, so I couldn't follow everything. But from what I gathered, there has been a problem with slinkers riding on The Train again." Sela pursed her lips.

"Slinkers are, how shall I say this, unwanted passengers. In Ugara, we might call them tramps. But that's not quite right either. Slinkers shouldn't be here. Sometimes they have an expired ticket—they didn't get off when they were supposed to. Or they never had a ticket at all, just snuck onto The Train, though that hardly seems possible. Otherwise, I believe they come up from second or third-class, trying to sneak into more comfortable positions, even though they don't have a valid ticket for it."

"But what do they do?" Rinatta persisted, hanging on every word. "What's a slinker do? Slink?"

Sela chuckled. "I'm not sure how they got that name. I guess because they're supposed to be very sneaky. Respectable passengers like us, we rarely see them. They just slide by, as if they're invisible. From what I understood, they mostly come out at night and try and sleep in people's compartments while we sleep in our beds."

Eli, about to take a sip from her own water cup, choked. She coughed noisily, as Willin stared unbelievingly at Sela. "Why they don't sleep in their bed?" he queried.

Sela shrugged. "I guess they don't have a bed, so our chairs seem better than the floor or a hard bench."

"They sleep on the floor?" Rinatta squealed. "Do they have a blanket?"

Eli gulped her water, trying to stifle more coughs. It gave her an excuse to hide her surprise.

That sandy-haired man. Lucca. She had definitely met a slinker. No wonder he had been so eager to get out of Big Trouble!

"What do they do if they catch a slinker? What will that man do to one?" Rinatta wondered.

"Kill him to death!" Three-year-old Willin's blood-and-guts phase responded instantly.

"Most likely." Sela sighed. "It's not a safe life. If they catch you slinking, I believe the punishment is death. And I imagine hiding around The Train all day is dangerous, too. But don't expect to see any slinkers. They're not like us. They're bad people."

After her brief encounters, Eli wasn't convinced that Lucca was bad. Reckless, certainly. Maybe he wasn't a very good slinker yet. After all, she'd seen him twice now! Perhaps he'd be more careful from here on, with these extra warnings against slinkers. She doubted she'd run into him again.

Sela brushed crumbs off of Rinatta's shirt. "You must eat more neatly," she said. "A Baroness minds each bite. It gives her strength and she does not let any go to waste."

Rinatta sucked in her breath. "Mama's the Baroness, not me. I'm never going to be like her. I never even see her. How should I know how she eats?" The last bit came out in a high-pitched whine, as Rinatta waited for Sela to scold her.

But the old woman only looked at the girl. She was silent a long time. "You are as she is," she said at last.

Rinatta's lower lip trembled. She wasn't sure what Sela meant. Her arms crossed rebelliously, but she didn't respond.

Another conductor entered the dining car. He held a plastic cone to his mouth, shouting in several languages. Finally, Eli caught the Sao Lindros dialect. She could just make it out. "Elduran!" he was calling. "Next stop is Elduran! Come out and stretch your legs, folks!"

The other passengers sighed in relief and many began to get up from the table. This was welcome news after the last announcement.

Pria leaned across the table and put her hand on Eli's shoulder, using The Traintalk word for "*Come!*"

Eli unbuckled the children from their booster seats. "Will you come too, Sela?" she asked.

The older woman shook her head. "No, the Baroness needs me." Eli had hoped she would stay to help her with Traintalk. "You can take the children out onto the platform. Don't stray too far," Sela told her. "It will be fun for them to see some new place."

"All right. Come on, you two. Let's go with Pria!" Eli ushered the children after the plump woman.

The Train was beginning to slow down. Eli could hear gears grinding squeakily to break its speed. They pulled into the station moments later.

Conductors hopped down, opening the side doors and unfolding boxes into the portable steps. Then they cleared the way for the passengers to get down.

As they came out, Eli heard Willin gasp. Stepping onto the platform, she looked where he was pointing.

The Train itself had changed. It was more streamlined now, its sides covered in steel plating. Red and blue stripes ran along the cars. The morning sun blazed down on The Train, making it shine against a tremendous blue sky.

But the weather was pleasantly mild, warmth without the nasty humidity that she would have felt on a day like this in Ugara.

Beyond the station, a great valley opened before them. Mountains loomed high in the east, gray and absolute, against the green of Elduran. It was a beautiful city, buildings sprawling close along stone roads, but with big squares of land for the trees to grow together. Eli didn't see any patches cleared for cows or goats. Eldurans had to make their living from something other than livestock.

Metal spyglasses were mounted at the edge of the platform. People lined up to take a look. A yellow sign posted on the railing showed a monkey in a tree. Eli took Rinatta and Willin over and waited for a turn at monkey-spotting. Pria showed the children how to close one eye and peep through the end. Rinatta was better at it than her brother.

"Ooh, I see one!" she yelled gleefully, aiming her spyglass at a tree at the bottom of the platform.

Eli managed to keep Willin from either shoving his sister out of the way in his impatience or climbing over the railing for a better look himself. She didn't want his impersonation of a monkey to get too realistic.

Pria's laughter was honey-gold. She began chattering in Traintalk, acting out her words to help Eli understand. She pointed to herself and pantomimed rocking a baby. Then she raised her arms high, marking the air above her head, to show her children were now grown taller than her.

Eli laughed too, enjoying the woman's easy manner and trying to speak more and more Traintalk, hoping to make it stick.

Pria pointed at Eli and the children, who were still monkey-spotting. "*You all*," she said. "*Bad place?*"

She seemed to be asking if they had come from a bad place. Perhaps Ugara would seem terrible to a Train rider, but Eli could only shrug. "Bou *bad*. But also bou *good*."

"Ah!" Pria shook her head and waved in the direction of the valley. Her hand swept back and forth to show the vastness of it all. "*Bad land. Bad Lands*."

"Bad Lands?" Eli repeated.

"*Sim!*" Pria confirmed. "*No good magic*." She grinned and twinkled her fingers as if casting a spell. "*No good smarts*." She pointed to her head, to her brain. Then, frowning, she held her palms close together, small and narrow. "*Bad Lands. In between*."

Seeing Eli still looking confused, she flapped the fingers on one hand off to the side of her dumpy body. "*Here. Good magics lands*." She then waved the opposite hand. "*Over here. Good smart lands*." Her hands went back to the middle. "*Here the Bad Lands. Nothing good. Nothing strong*." She made muscles, causing Eli to giggle again.

"Yes, that's Ugara all right, too." Eli spoke in Ugaran, nodding to show she agreed. She knew Ugara and the areas around it were a nothing-spot with no stations. Now she saw why. The Train had no reason to stop in a place with so little magic and so little technology. Sure, they had a few charms and enough conveniences to get by. But nothing that compared to smart sinks and toilets! She wondered what she would see in a place where magic was strong.

"*The Train*," Pria touched her smiling lips, "*always good place*."

A conductor began calling for them to re-board The Train. Eli showed him her ticket, but he barely glanced at it before waving them aboard. She supposed she could not be suspected of slinking, not with two little ones in tow. They'd be impossible to hide.

As they went back to their seats in their compartment, Eli felt The Train begin to move. Its wheels clenched tight against the tracks, rolling round and round, faster and faster. Her eyes got used to the blur of trees outside their window. But she could feel the Railroad sloping upward, carrying them closer to the mountains on the far side of Elduran.

After a few hours, The Train stopped again, at a station called Winitar. It waited there just long enough for passengers to get on or off. After that, The Train stopped every few hours. They seemed to be in a busy stretch of the Railroad.

They passed through a long tunnel and the night-lighting came on for a little while. On the other side, the trees grew farther from each other, while the earth yellowed and turned rocky and hard. By evening they came into the mountains. The Railroad cut into their side, going up and up. Thinking of the workers back home, Eli tried to imagine the mountain men coming out from their homes to lay the tracks.

After dinner, Eli took the children to get clean. All the shower stalls were being used, so they had to wait. Willin and Rinatta usually took baths. They didn't enjoy getting blasted with water from above. She had better luck adjusting the temperature this time, but Willin flailed and cried when soap got in his eyes. She ended up having to take off her clothes and get in the stall with them—it was crowded, but she had more control. She gave her own hair a quick rinse so she wouldn't have to shower again in the morning.

She bundled the children into bed. The Train slowed down for another stop. Conductors called out. Before she knew it, she was asleep again.

The days passed, swift as The Train's motion. Beyond the mountains were low hills, then fields. After these came new jungles, broken up into stretches between busy towns.

Eli, who was good at deciphering Toddlertalk, found that she followed the flow of Traintalk with similar ease. She had supposed it would be too hard for the children to learn a new language—surely, they were too little. To her amazement, they soaked it up even faster. She soon found herself chattering back and forth with them in a broken mixture of Ugaran grammar with as many Traintalk words thrown in as they could think of.

Most of Eli's time was spent with the children in the compartment or taking them on walks around The Train. She tried to get them to leave other travelers alone, but didn't mind letting them wander through the passenger and dining cars.

The mossy green carpeting ran through first-class, but after that became a swirly flowered print. Second-class did not have private compartments. Instead, the passengers had to sit in rows and rows of seats that didn't even face each other. At least the chairs looked comfortable, with individual armrests and backs that reclined. There were a lot more families in second-class, even women with babies. Parents tended to stay in their seats, while letting their children gather in little gangs to scamper among the rows and play spotting games out the windows.

Eli tried to relax her need to keep an eye on her charges every second and let Rinatta go over to a small group of kids. But after a short time the girl came back, angrily tossing her braids.

"They're just a bunch of babies," she reported, and made no more attempts to join them.

Eli didn't dare go down to third-class with the children. Her Traintalk wasn't good enough yet, and she was worried they would stand out too much.

Indeed, despite her best efforts, having the only youngsters in first-class drew plenty of attention. In the carriage, it was easier to keep them reined in, but meal times were another matter. With a dining car's worth of noise to compete against, Rinatta and Willin defaulted to their own top volume. The other passengers exchanged sympathetic looks with Eli and then whispered to each other when her back was turned.

Occasionally, Eli spared herself the daily embarrassment by ordering meals from one of the snack-sellers who went up and down the aisles. Some pushed carts, while others carried trays of delicious treats. They cheerfully accepted small chunks of salt crystal from her, and she could eat in the privacy of their own compartment.

Sela usually joined them in the dining car, but that didn't help much. As usual, she left the childcare up to Eli and spent her time in making small talk with the other passengers. Eli's rapidly growing Traintalk wasn't enough for adult conversation.

Of the Baroness, Eli saw little. After breakfast, Sela had Eli bring the children into compartment seventeen, where she gave them their lessons. Sometimes the Baroness was there, but more often it was just Sela and the children. Strangely, no other passengers shared that compartment. Eli wondered if this was a stroke of good luck for the reclusive older women, or if it had been planned. She hadn't noticed the Baroness making any special demands when she bought their tickets, but who knew?

During their morning lessons, Sela made the children practice Traintalk with her and showed them maps of the Railroad. She made them study the names of the families that belonged to the Great Houses that founded the Railroad, sang songs and rhymes about its construction and made them chant the names of stations they were coming up on: Kambok, Pingaspor, Namila, Liho...

That hour of lessons was Eli's only official time off. She could sit in, if she chose, but no matter how interesting she found Sela's knowledge of The Train, she often needed the break. She found she learned as much exploring by herself in that hour. She enjoyed going on walks or practicing her own

Traintalk with Pria. The plump woman and her husband were both retired professors, who had given up their homeland to travel round the world. They'd been going round and round for several years now, Eli learned, and had no intention of getting off.

It was interesting that some passengers had a set destination in mind, while others rode for the sake of riding. But for all those who traveled, it was more than a means of transportation, more than a home: it was a way of life. Every day, moving forward, moving on.

Servers bustled up and down the aisle, heading to the dining car to set out the midday meal. Eli, having spent her free hour wandering The Train, made her way back to their compartments.

Standing outside the door, she could hear Willin's voice ringing out, high and shrill. "When's lunch? When's Eli going to be here?"

"Sela, I'm bored now. Can we be done?" Rinatta whined.

Chuckling, Eli reached for the handle to relieve them of their tiny misery.

Suddenly, the doors at the back of the car opened. The Baroness Vasri came in and stalked up the aisle toward her compartment.

Funny, thought Eli. *I can hardly remember seeing her out and about on The Train before. She never wants to have anything to do with the other riders. What does she do when she's not with Sela? Where does she go? Where has she been?*

Then the car doors closer to her banged open. Three conductors rushed into the narrow corridor. The rat-faced man stood out in front. He carried a short, black stick. "Sim," he breathed. "That's definitely her."

The men were looking down the aisle, right at the Baroness Vasri.

Eli had never seen the Baroness lose her cool, collected manner. But for a moment, when she saw the conductors, a gray, haunted look passed over her face. Then the Baroness looked angry, very angry. She turned around and began to walk back up the aisle, the way she'd come.

"Stop right there!" yelled the conductor.

Three more blue-coated men burst in through the back doors. They blocked the Baroness' path. Slowly, she turned around again to face the rat-man.

"Very well," she said. "We can do this the hard way." As she spoke, she didn't meet his eyes. She seemed to look past him, at the wall. Not looking at Eli. But somehow the not-looking, Eli felt, was directed right at her.

Eli pressed herself up against the compartment's wall. The conductors were so intent on the Baroness, none of them seemed to care about her.

"Anya Vashani?" the conductor asked. The Baroness nodded, once. "You are a known partner of that great traitor, Director Mehra. By the judgment of the Railroad Barons, you are charged with treason against the Railroad and for the crime of re-boarding after Exile from The Train."

Eli couldn't believe what she was hearing. The Baroness made no attempt to deny his accusations.

"You must come with us now." The conductor pushed her shoulder to get her to start walking.

"Where will you take me?" asked the Baroness, coolly, still not-looking right at Eli.

"This is still The Train," the conductor said, his eyes sharp and suspicious. "We abide by the law. You will wait in the holding car until we arrive in Dongorland." He jerked his arm stiffly. "This way."

The conductors marched the Baroness out the back of the car.

Shaking, Eli opened the door to compartment seventeen.

"You're here—" Eli stopped Rinatta and Willin's cheers with a sharp gesture. She was sure her face looked ghastly. She could barely contain her shock.

"What's the matter, child?" asked Sela, concerned.

"The Baroness." Eli gulped. "Didn't you hear? The conductors took her." She didn't want to alarm the children, but this was too serious to hide.

A calculating look crossed Sela's face. "I see. Go on."

"Just now, outside in the aisle. They took her. The man said she committed treason against the Railroad Barons." Eli repeated the charges as best as she could remember. "They took her to a holding car."

Sela snorted. "That fool! I told her it was too dangerous for her to go out. People on The Train have long memories."

"Is Mama in jail?" demanded Rinatta.

"Only because she is a useless idiot," sighed the old woman. Eli had never heard Sela speak ill of her mistress before. "It won't take them long to realize I was helping her. They'll come for me next, and whoever else she traveled with. Children, Eli, listen to me very carefully. I won't be able to help you. You'll have to be on your own. Those men, those conductors, must not find you. You must keep riding The Train until we reach Dongorland."

"We have to hide?" gasped Rinatta.

"Hide and seek?" queried Willin, looking scared.

"No, stupid!" Rinatta shot back.

"Shut up," snapped Sela, and they fell silent. "Children, stay with Eli and do exactly what she tells you. Do not trust anyone else. It's not safe on The Train for you anymore."

"Where should we go?" faltered Eli, scared almost spitless.

"You need to get the children to the Dongor station," repeated Sela. "Rinatta, Willin, you will find friends there. The new director of the Rassa House will meet you at the station. Then you will have the power to free us." She sighed in frustration. "We were so close, it's within five days' journey. You have to keep away from the conductors. Don't let them see you. Don't let them check your tickets—they'll be looking for you. Try and move down to second or third-class—it'll be more crowded, but it's easier to be overlooked, even with these two. I guess that's a place to start, but keep moving. You're a clever girl, Eli. You'll find a way."

Sela's face was grave, her voice low. The old woman's hands shook, but she stood up and rummaged in one of her bags.

She drew out a cloth pouch. "I hoped that we might complete our journey unnoticed, but I knew this was a possibility. I put a little money, a few supplies together for you. There's some food—not much, I'm afraid, but it could last you a few days."

She squeezed Rinatta's hand, then grabbed Willin's and brought it to her lips for a kiss. "Be brave, be good, little ones." Looking over at Eli, she tried to smile. "Go. Now. They are coming."

Eli's heart hammered, but she fought down the spiraling feeling of horror. "Come on, children," she heard herself saying as she opened the door.

"What about lunch?" squeaked Willin.

"Shut up!" hissed Rinatta, and he fell silent.

They stepped out into the aisle. Eli hesitated, then led the children down through the accordion doors.

She started to shove the doors to open the way to the next car, but froze. A team of conductors were making their way up through the car's aisle.

"Never mind," Eli muttered. "Let's not go this way." Gritting her teeth, she hustled them back the way they had come, back through their own car. Where now? She doubted she could get all the way down the long aisle to the doors on the other end. Not before those conductors burst in and spotted them.

Thinking fast, Eli decided to duck into her own compartment. Maybe they'd stop for Sela first and give her a chance to slip out while they were distracted.

"Come on in here. Just for a minute." Eli got the children through and closed the door as quickly as she could. *I'm panicking. Don't panic. There's no time for it.*

Pria and Nassan were in the compartment. Nassan had gone over onto Eli's side again, to have more space for his long legs. He quickly got up, bowing an apology.

"*Kei kei*, Eli. Children." Pria greeted them, then saw their faces. "Good heavens, what's wrong?"

Eli heard feet marching down the hall outside, then stop at the door across from their compartment. Sela. They'd come for Sela.

"They're looking for us," she blurted out. She wasn't supposed to tell them—she wasn't supposed to trust anyone. But she couldn't do it alone. She didn't know how. "They're trying to take us away. I don't know what to do. We're supposed to hide."

Nassan and Pria exchanged startled glances.

"Did you do something wrong?" gasped Pria.

"No, not anything! At least, not us. But they think we did. I'm not sure." Her voice squeaked helplessly and she had to stop talking. She didn't want Willin and Rinatta to catch her panic.

"You must have done something to upset them. This is serious, Eli. Breaking Train rules—" began Pria.

"Of course she didn't."

Eli was surprised to hear Nassan speak on her behalf. He shook his head. "It is impossible. I have seen her. She does right by these children."

"Well—" Pria frowned, hesitating.

They could hear raised voices coming from the compartment opposite theirs.

"Oh, please," gasped Eli. "They'll look here next, I'm sure of it."

"Stand back," ordered Nassan, ushering Eli and the children closer to the window. He cracked the door and peered out into the aisle.

"Sir! Stay in your compartment, sir! This is a matter of Train security," snapped a man's voice.

Was Sela putting up a fight? Maybe she was trying to create a distraction or delay the conductors so Eli could get farther away. *Too bad we're trapped right next door. All they have to do is look inside and they'll find us. I've failed already.*

Nassan shut the door. He stroked his beard, then raised one finger. "Very well, hide here until they move on."

Glumly, Eli looked around at the six seats. A few children's toys and blankets were tossed about, as well as some rolls of parchment that Pria had been reading. The chairs were built into the wall, with not enough room underneath to hide in, and the ceiling space was taken up by their luggage racks. There were no hidden corners or nooks.

Eli took a deep breath. She could hear the rush of The Train, feel its steady, constant flow under her feet as it rolled down the tracks. For some reason, its now-familiar rhythm, the sound of the tracks, helped clear her wits.

Darting forward, she scrambled on top of the cushiony seat. She took a firm hold of the luggage rack, testing the sturdiness of the brass frame. Yes. It had to be strong, to hold all those heavy bags. People were expected to travel with their entire lives here.

She tugged at their bags, trying to get them down, to make some room.

Nassan rushed to help her. He was stronger and taller and quickly cleared some space. Then he moved to the other side, clearing out his own belongings, as well as the Ahns'.

Eli knelt next to Rinatta. "You know how we sometimes play the Quiet Game?" The little girl nodded. "This is going to be like that. Some men will come and look in here, and you can't let them see you up there. Can you do that?"

Rinatta gave her a haughty look. "'Course. It'll be easy. I'm not a baby."

I wish I were that confident.

Eli hoisted Rinatta up onto the first rack. The girl inched her way to the back and lay down.

"Willin and I will be right on the other side. Don't look for us. Just stay as quiet as you can."

Rinatta gave her a determined nod. "I can do it."

Eli and Nassan packed some of the bags back in around Rinatta until she was completely hidden.

Nassan had to give Eli a boost to get her up onto the other rack. It didn't even creak under her weight, which was reassuring. Tucking in her legs, she lay down across the bars. They were set close together, but there were still awkward gaps between them. The cold metal pressed hard against her. Nassan lifted Willin up and she pulled him close to lie flat against her body. The boy whimpered, scared and confused.

Moving with surprising speed, Nassan arranged the suitcases around her. Some of them jutted off the edge of the rack now. Eli hoped no one would notice they weren't placed back as far as they should be.

"I can still see Eli's feet," warned Pria.

"Cover them with a blanket," came a muffled voice from the other rack.

"Excellent idea, Rinatta," Nassan praised her.

"That's how I always beat Willin at hide-and-seek," returned the girl. "If part of you sticks out, you have to cover it up."

"I see," said Nassan. "Now, it must be like you are no longer here." There was a rustle of papers as he arranged himself on the seat.

Silence.

Willin whimpered again. "Shhhh," Eli hugged him close to her, pressing a finger over his lips to try to squelch any sounds. He was struggling not to cry. Unlike his sister, he wasn't following what was going on. Too many adults saying too many things.

Voices outside.

Someone rapped at the door and opened it.

"The girl who looks after the children. Have you seen them?" demanded a man. Eli had no trouble recognizing the rat-faced man's voice.

"They were here a few minutes ago," answered Pria, innocently. "She said she was taking them to the dining car."

Eli held her breath. There was a stretch of silence. Would he search the room? What if he decided to confiscate all their belongings?

"Very well," said the conductor at last. "If they return, report it right away to a conductor. They are no longer allowed to travel on The Train."

The door opened again—he was leaving!

Willin sneezed.

Eli clapped her hand over his face, trying to muffle any other sounds that the boy might make. He squirmed uncomfortably.

The door creaked again and held; he wasn't leaving. Eli's heart sank. She could hear the soft sound of his feet as he turned around.

"Ahhhhh, are you hungry my pet?" exclaimed Nassan, out of nowhere. "Yes, I can see. You are ready for snacks. Come, I have fresh banana." He started looking for the fruit jar to feed his lizard. Eli guessed he was making extra noise to cover up any more sounds from the children.

The conductor lingered a moment longer. Finally, Eli heard the wonderful sound of the door closing.

They waited a few minutes. Eli's ears strained for footsteps outside, trying to make sure he was actually walking away. Willin trembled against her. She stroked his arm. It was an awkward motion, but his body relaxed against her touch.

"He has gone. Do you wish to stay hidden or come down?" Nassan's quiet voice drifted up to them.

"Ugh. Down, please," said Eli. They needed to get out before that conductor came back.

Nassan cleared away the bags and helped them get out. Rinatta sprang down into his arms. "We won!"

"Yes! We did it!" Eli congratulated them, as if they had really been playing a game. "We have to get ready to go now." She figured that, since the conductor had just left, she might have a few minutes until he decided to check back. She opened the children's luggage and began stuffing extra clothes and nappies into her rucksack, along with the supplies Sela had given her.

Pria was frowning uncertainly. "Are you sure this is wise, Eli? You are breaking the law. Perhaps there has been some mistake and it just needs to be cleared up. You should go to them and explain."

"I suppose." Eli hesitated, thinking. "The conductor, he arrested the Baroness, the children's mother. But he called the wrong name. He said she was someone called Anya Vashani. But she didn't deny it, so it must be true. I can't risk it. I'm supposed to keep the children safe."

Pria's eyes widened. "Vashani?"

"I think so, yes. Why?" Eli looked up to see the other woman's face turned pale as bone. "Do you know that name?"

Pria and Nassan exchanged a worried glance.

"I'm afraid so," Pria said. "The Vashani House is one of the oldest Railroad Baronies. Not one of the Founding Families, who laid the first tracks, but they joined The Train soon after that. Powerful magic users long ago, but there weren't many Vashanis left. Just a small clan. They had lost much of their wealth, you see. They were still respected, that is, until—"

Pria broke off, frowning uncertainly.

"Go on," Eli prompted.

"It was a few years ago. I still remember it well, it was talked over, all over The Train. First class, third class, everyone heard about it. The remaining members of the Vashani clan were sent into Exile."

"Exile where?" asked Eli.

"To—to the Bad Lands. Where you came from. Where nothing is good." She lowered her eyes. "I'm sorry. It must be true. It is a great crime to return after Exile from The Train."

"But what happened? Why were they sent away?"

Nassan spoke: "I don't know the details. The Railroad Barons—there are many great Houses. They keep the Railroad going. They appoint officials and workers, and see to the tracks. There are matters of policy. And payments. Some Houses are strong, others not so strong. Some are old, like the Vashanis; that counts too. There is a, a delicate balance of power between the Houses. It's business to them. They deal in business with each other, yes, but also in life. There are marriages between the families, making the Houses greater and bigger. Other times there are great wars."

"Did the Vashani clan lose a war, then?" Eli asked.

Pria nodded. "A business war. The director of the Vashani clan tried to take over House Rassa. An unwanted move by the other Houses. Since the Vashanis acted without the other Barons' approval, they were cast out. They may no longer travel the Railroad, or live near towns where The Train stops."

"I guess that explains why they came to Ugara." Eli sighed. "That's so far from any station, sometimes it even feels like Exile to the people who live there."

"I wonder what would make your Baroness want to come back?" said Nassan. "So dangerous, it could cost her life or her children's."

Eli shrugged. "I don't know if she'd even think about something like that. At least Sela cares. At least she knows that children don't have anything to do with Train Houses and Railroad laws."

Pria did not agree. "Oh, Eli, out here, it doesn't work that way. They share the same blood. Bloodlines are very important to The Train families. They are meticulous about things like that."

"It's not fair," muttered Eli.

Nassan chuckled and gestured to Rinatta and Willin, who were sitting quietly, staring at the grown ups. "You sound more like one of them."

"Well, someone has to be on their side!" Eli sprang up. "Come on, kids, let's go!"

"Here." Nassan handed her his jar of fruit. "It's not much."

"Thanks." Eli smiled at him.

Pria's hands fluttered, a little nervous movement, like candle flame. "I am sorry, Eli. I don't know what I can do. We, that is, Uma and I, we saved everything to have this chance, to come to The Train. We can't—I can't—"

"I get it," said Eli, smoothing over the woman's fears. "You won't have to lie for us again. We'll stay away."

She couldn't be angry with Pria for being afraid to help fugitives. Instead, she hugged the woman good-bye. After Nassan had checked the hall to make sure it was empty, they took off.

Eli led the children down to one of the second-class cars.

There were three open seats on one side of the aisle. It was hard to be sure if they were free, perhaps their riders were using the lavatory car. Eli put Willin in her lap and sank into an empty spot.

Was everyone looking at them? Did people remember her from earlier walks through The Train? Had she taken someone's seat?

No. To her relief, the other passengers barely glanced at her. They kept sitting, staring at the chairs in front of them. They hardly bothered to look out the window.

A baby started crying a few rows back.

"I'm hungry," Willin said. "We didn't have lunch, Eli."

Fortunately, second-class was the favorite territory for the snack-sellers, with their baskets and carts. Eli bought bowls of fried noodles and vegetables, which the children gobbled up enthusiastically. She choked down some of hers. The bowl came with a cardboard lid she could fold over the top to prevent spills—and to save the rest for later.

The children relaxed once they'd eaten. They spent the afternoon playing in their new seats.

"We must look for spies," insisted Rinatta, crouching low.

"Yeah, no bad guys," agreed Willin. "I'll shoot 'em. Bang!" He curled his fingers into the shape of a gun and blasted his sister.

"Willin shooted me!" she squawked. "You shoot bad guys."

Eli rolled her eyes. She'd never been a big fan of shooting games, but they came so naturally, she couldn't squash them out. At least this one made the children feel powerful. She didn't want to take that away right now.

Instead, she played along. "All right, troopers. Our new mission is to stay low so the bad guys can't track our location. Any conductors may be collaborating with the enemy, so we need to stay away until we reach our rendezvous point." She sounded ridiculous, but they loved it.

"I wish we had spyglasses, like for monkey-spotting," sighed Rinatta, poking her head out to scan up and down the aisle.

They didn't seem bothered by their mother's absence: it was nothing unusual. Even though Rinatta had followed that the Baroness was taken away by the conductors, she didn't seem upset. Willin was easily distracted, but remained on the fussy side. Eli knew he was anxious, not sure what was going on.

They passed an uncomfortable night. The second-class lavatory car had a long wait. Willin and Rinatta wanted to go back to their beds, and were grumpy about having to sleep in the chairs.

Eli sang her soothe-song, but the charm hardly seemed to have an effect here. *We're passing through the smart lands*, Eli remembered. *It's just a lullaby here. I wonder what will happen if I sing where magic is strong?*

She rocked Willin to settle him and he fell asleep in her lap. She figured out the buttons to make her chair recline and positioned him more comfortably. Rinatta sprawled out horizontally, draping her feet onto the armrest of Willin's chair.

Eli didn't dare sleep. She mustn't. What if a conductor came by, on patrol, and spotted them? Or came to check their tickets and realized they were in the wrong car? They could be grabbed for slinking first, and then their connection to the Baroness would come out.

At some point, she must have drifted off. When she woke up, the early dawn glow filled The Train. Unlike the curtained bed of the sleeper car, the second-class windows only had thin blinds that you could pull up and down, and the sunlight behind them was white and warm.

Letting Willin sleep on top of her was a terrible idea. She was sore and his weight had made all her limbs go numb. She managed to sit up and roll him into the chair next to her. He snuffled thickly, but didn't even open his eyes.

Now that she was awake, she felt the fear again. How long would they be safe here? Should they move again?

Trying to shake the tingling feeling from her arms and feet, she lifted the blinds and peered out.

The sun shone clear and bright against a sky streaked with violet and gray clouds. Instead, it was the ground—no, the water—that reflected blue. Waves crested and broke like falling stars in the water below the tracks. The shoreless horizon looked cold and lonely. Eli shivered. She had never seen the ocean before.

Yet The Train glided over the sea. She couldn't tell how much of the Railroad they crossed and how much fell away behind them. The bridge went on and on.

Slowly, in a manner to which they were accustomed, the other passengers in the car began to rise for the day. Many of them paused to look out the window, nodding in appreciation: at last they had come to the sea.

And so they rode, all morning, until a voice over a speaker blared out, "Liho! Next stop is Liho! Train stops here to reload."

The Train slowed and began to approach its next station, an island rising suddenly out of the deep. Clouds hung like tarnished silver above the platform, and soon a light drizzle of rain began. Still, most of the passengers went out to stretch their legs.

This seemed like the perfect chance to look for a new hiding spot.

"Let's check on third-class," suggested Eli. "We've never been there before. It won't be so crowded with everyone getting off." *And we can pretend we're new passengers who just got on. Less chance of being recognized.*

But when they went back there, Eli wasn't so sure it was a good plan after all. Instead of individual seats, there were only hard, wooden benches for the passengers to sit on. Many travelers had left their possessions on board, marking their spots with baskets of toiletries or a pillow to sit on. Rinatta and Willin scampered up and down, eagerly exploring.

"Which seat numbers are for us?" asked Rinatta.

"I'm not sure. I think we have to wait until the other passengers come back. We'll see what's free after they all sit down." Eli planned out loud.

"What if they're all full? Or what if there's not room for us to be together?"

Eli hadn't thought of that. "Well, we'll sit as close as we can, then. Or Willin can sit on my lap again."

"Ugh, it'll be worse than the carriage ride," the girl complained.

The windows were lowered partway here, and a cool, salt breeze whipped through the car. Someone was coming up the stairs on the platform.

A conductor entered. He noticed them right away, and looked surprised. "Can I help you, Miss?"

Eli tried to keep her face calm. "Uh, no. We're fine, thanks."

"I'm surprised you didn't want to take your—" He paused and took a closer look at Eli and Rinatta's faces, trying to guess their ages. "—sister and brother out to the station. They'd enjoy it."

"She's not our sister," laughed Willin.

"Oh. I'm sorry," he said sincerely. "Here now, which are your seats?"

Eli gulped. "Actually, we're just on our way to the lavatory car," she improvised, slinging her rucksack across her shoulders. "Hurry up guys, let's go."

"But I don't hafta go!" exclaimed Rinatta.

"Well, I do. Now." Eli hustled them to the door.

Laughing, the conductor started to turn away. Then he stopped. "Hey! Wait a minute! You're that nanny, aren't you? The nanny from first-class?"

Eli scooped up Willin into the crook of her arm. "Run!" she yelled to Rinatta.

The girl didn't need to be told twice. She took off down the aisle ahead of Eli.

"Come back!" shouted the conductor. "Stop right there!" He paused in confusion, then dashed after them.

Eli forgot her aching arms and legs and that Willin was getting too big to be carried for long. She ran, and nothing else mattered.

They burst through doors, dashing through the cars. Back, up through second-class. The carriage doors were open, and a group of passengers were coming up the steps to return to their seats, jabbering in mixtures of Traintalk and other languages.

Eli caught the sound of other conductors shouting from the station: "All aboard!"

She gave Rinatta a quick shove, hurrying her past just as The Train riders started to come in. They crowded up the aisle, having to go down to single file to get their seats.

"Keep going," Eli panted to Rinatta.

The conductor rushed up, but he was caught in the surge of people. "Out of the way. Out of the way!" Eli could hear him yelling and then cursing their clumsiness.

She didn't stop to look back. She ran on, making her way up to the other second-class car, the one she had been riding in that morning.

Passengers were taking their seats here too. She had to slow down—there wasn't room—she couldn't run any more. They needed a place to hide before he caught up. There wasn't even a full car-length between them.

By the carriage doors, she noticed a man in black, with tan ankle boots. Trying to look as if he were not waiting around, but not wandering off either, it was Lucca the slinker.

She grabbed Rinatta's hand and they rushed up to him.

"Lucca!" She tried to catch her breath. "We need to hide. Help us!"

He started, taking in her flushed face and the scared children. "Er, I think you are mistaking me for someone else, miss," he said, smiling crookedly while he started to sidle away.

Eli wouldn't let him weasel out. She blocked his path. "I know what you are." He hesitated, so she pressed on: "The conductors are after us. I know you can get around them. That's what you do, right?"

He twisted his lips, but didn't reply.

A whistle blew behind them. The conductor was at the back of the car now.

"Make way. Train business! Make way!"

Lucca grinned. "Follow me, kiddos," he said.

Where was there to go? Nowhere, but into the next car. They hurried forward, back in first-class, but a conductor already stood there, guiding passengers to their seats.

Lucca had other ideas, though. He marched them over to the carriage doors and down the steps.

"Wait!" gasped Eli. "We need to stay on The Train!"

"Don't worry!" he called over his shoulder. "I never miss a ride."

They darted along the platform, passing the cars they had already run through. The rain had stopped and the last few passengers were hurrying toward The Train, ready to board.

Lucca stopped at the first boxcar. On the side, a steel ladder was mounted.

"Hop on up," he said.

Willin stared. "Where does it go?"

"On top. Great view from up there." He started to climb up. "Here, I'll help you. Have a go."

"You're crazy!" exclaimed Eli.

"You were crazy enough to ask me for help," he returned. "Don't worry, come up and see!"

Eli watched Willin and Rinatta clamber up the ladder and Lucca helped pull them up onto the roof of the car. Then she climbed up herself. It was high.

On top of the car, someone had secured planks to act as a little fence, surrounding half the roof. It was only a few feet high, but enough to rest against one's back, if he was sitting down. Looking about, Eli saw that there were little metal handholds around the sides. A few bags and a trunk were tied down with twine.

"Welcome aboard, my new friends!" laughed Lucca and The Train began to move.

The Train sounds came louder and sharper than ever. The whistle blared, the wheels surged forward. She could feel the boxcar swaying to and fro much more than she had ever noticed from inside.

"Is this dangerous?" she yelped.

"Sure, but you'll get used to it," replied Lucca. "Use the handles if you're worried."

Rinatta and Willin were sitting toward the middle, their bodies rocking unsteadily. Eli beckoned for them to crawl over to her and got each one to grab a handle in the fence. Ahead, she could see they were leaving the island. The bridge that ran over the sea continued on. The wind whipped in their faces, burning cold and sharp against their skin.

Lucca crawled over to the trunk with a well-practiced air. He thumbed the combination to the lock and began unfolding a large tarp and screwing together plastic tubes into a pole. He set the pole in the middle of the car and clipped the sides of tarp to each corner of the fence. With everyone sitting down, it just covered the adults' heads, like a little tent.

"It will still be cold, but this keeps the spray out. It's not my favorite time to ride up here, not when we're crossing the ocean."

Lucca also produced some large sheets of silver foil. "These will keep you warm." He shoved them over to Eli; she realized they were blankets.

"I've never seen anything like this," she said, helping Rinatta and Willin get wrapped up.

"They're not pretty, but they work. Especially at night." Lucca handed Eli the last blanket and sat back comfortably.

"Don't you need one?" asked Rinatta.

"Nah," said the slinker.

They were rolling onto the sea-bridge now. Eli could hear the waves crashing below, and water splashed the tarp. It slid off the tent.

Willin regarded Lucca with great respect. "What this place?" he wanted to know.

"We call it the blindman's nest. You said you needed a safe spot, and this is one of the best. Conductors never know of it, and Train folk never see it."

"Safe being a relative term, I expect," mutter Eli. "What if you fall off?"

"I wouldn't recommend staying in the nest when you go through a tunnel. I've heard that even if slinkers lie flat, they might not come out the other side. And you don't want to be up here when we pull into a station; it's too special a place to risk. But as long as you have a sure foot and keep your wits about you, it's a fine way to travel. You can spend the day staring up at the sky and you feel like a cloud just sailing along."

Eli shuddered and wrapped the blanket closer. But she thought she should remember her manners. "Thank you for bringing us up here. I'm pretty sure you saved us," she said.

"It turns out I have a soft spot for a damsel in distress. Not to mention a couple of ragamuffins." He tweaked Rinatta's nose and she giggled. "But I sure wonder what you could be up to that would set a conductor's ass on fire."

"It's not just him," sighed Eli. "They're all looking for us by now."

"Problem with your tickets?" guessed Lucca.

"No." Eli wasn't sure how much to tell him. Maybe it would be better, the less he knew.

"It's our mama," Rinatta piped up. "She wasn't supposed to ride The Train. So they caught her and they're taking her to jail. We have to keep away or they'll lock us right up too."

Eli's mouth fell open, but Lucca was nodding seriously. "That's quite a problem. So now Miss—er, Eli, wasn't it?—is working hard to protect you. Do you have a plan?"

"Just, um, Sela, their mother's servant, said we need to keep going until we reach a station called Dongor. I hope someone will meet us there who can help."

"Did the servant tell you anything else?"

"Not really. She just gave us some supplies. I guess she knew this might happen. One of our compartment-mates said the Baroness's family had been Exiled because they lost a business war with another old Train family."

Lucca scratched his head, looking thoughtful. "I've been on the line for a couple years now, but I'm still a Road Kid to most of the other slinkers. I can't say I pay much attention to Train politics, but there's some of us that keep an eye on it for those that don't. Cerci might know more, if anyone would." He sighed. "There's a potluck tomorrow morning. I'll have to bring you along."

"Why is the pot lucky?" Rinatta wanted to know.

He chuckled. "Not that kind of pot. It's a party of sorts. We mostly slink on our own, but sometimes we like a little get-together. That way, we can share news and warnings. I've never seen anyone bring an outsider, but I get the feeling this is important." He scooted closer. "Got anything good in your backpack? Everyone throws in food or something."

"Not much." Eli was loathe to give away any of her supplies. But he was helping them...

She opened the rucksack. "I have a jar of fruit and some leftover noodles. And I think Sela gave us some food bars." She opened the pouch from the servant. There were a dozen food bars, each sealed in its own wrapper. She also saw smaller canvas bags tied with gold twine. Sela had given her what was left of the precious salt crystals.

At the bottom of the pouch were several rolled pieces of paper and two tiny bottles made of green glass.

Eli unrolled one of the papers. It was some sort of form, with boxes filled out in the Baroness' handwriting. But it was written in a script she couldn't recognize. Another paper had an illustration of the bottles at the top. The rest of the paper held no words, but a series of bars with numbers at the bottom. *Some sort of graph?* The bars were crossed at seemingly random points with little lines, some very thin, others thicker.

"Can you read any of this?" she asked Lucca. "I wonder if these are important."

Lucca reached for the first form. "I don't read very well," he admitted. "There's some numbers here. Three, five, eighteen. A lot of zeros…"

"That's Rinatta's birthday!" exclaimed Eli. "Maybe it's some sort of birth certificate?" One of the other papers had a matching form, filled out with Willin's birthday.

"How about these?" She showed Lucca the green bottles. They were empty, but each had a label stuck on the front.

Lucca shrugged. "Bring it tomorrow. You can show Cerci. She knows a lot. Not just about The Train, about the whole world."

Hours passed before Lucca deemed it time to go inside. They folded the blankets and took down the tent, making sure everything was stowed neatly. For the next slinker to use, Lucca explained.

They'd come to land again; the sun was starting to sink low. Lucca opened a trapdoor that lay just beyond the fenced-in part of the roof. Eli went down the rope ladder first. He helped the children along after her.

Willin stared at the crowded interior of the baggage car. "Look at all this stuff!"

"Don't touch any of it," said Lucca. "We're slinkers. Not thieves."

"But *we're* not slinkers!" responded Willin, shocked.

The young man laughed. "You are now. Riding around the Railroad, trying not to get caught. That's just like a slinker. Now, how would you like a real challenge? Let's find ourselves a good sleeping spot for the night."

Eli balked when he led them right back into first-class. "No way! Everyone will recognize us here. Plus, there's all kinds of warnings against slinkers. They put up signs in the dining car."

"Slinkers collect those signs," Lucca said airily. "Trust me, first-class is the best for slinking. All those lazy, rich passengers, going off to their beds, leaving all those soft chairs empty. It would be a crime not to sleep in them."

Once the night-lighting came on, the compartments emptied as people left for the night. Eli and her companions slipped back in.

Lucca explained the subtitles of slinking to them in a dramatic whisper: "We are night-creatures. Like shadows. Like wind. Like lightning striking before anyone knows."

Rinatta and Willin followed along easily, doing their best to mimic his panther-quiet steps.

Lucca found an empty compartment and they made themselves at home. A few leather suitcases on the racks. Other than that, little to identify whose seats they were taking. Eli wondered if they belonged to someone she'd recognize from the dining car.

Lucca jammed a bit of metal under the base of the door. "It won't hold off one of the crooks, but we'll wake up while he's rattling the door about," he said.

"Crooks?" repeated Rinatta.

"Conductors who chase slinkers. They'll Ditch you without a second thought. Throw you right off The Train—while it's still moving, mind you."

That sounded as bad as being jailed up like the Baroness and Sela!

But, oh, it certainly was nice to sink into those moss-green seats again! After their night in second-class and their cold day riding the roof, Eli couldn't stay awake any longer.

She opened her eyes some hours later, feeling surprisingly well rested. It was still night, but Lucca was sitting up. He looked at her, a deep, cool glance across the darkness.

"Is someone coming?" she whispered.

He shook his head. "No. But it's an hour until sunup. We should probably go."

Eli moved over to Willin and Rinatta's sleeping forms. How often had she given thanks for their nap times or when they fell asleep at the end of a chaotic day of Willin whining and Rinatta trying to boss everyone around? How they had surprised her these last few days, tiny powerhouses of courage and resilience! Gently, she brushed Willin's curls from his forehead. They were amazing.

"Amazing," murmured Lucca. She turned around. He was still looking at her. "I don't think I've ever met anyone on The Train like you."

"What do you mean?"

"Completely unselfish. You never even thought once about dumping this job, did you?"

"It's not a job. These are real people!" Did he think she was being brave? Well, maybe she was. Or maybe just stupid.

Making sure everything was as they had found it, they got the kids up and slipped out into the hall.

The slinkers' meeting was in the laundry car. That seemed an odd choice to Eli, but Lucca explained that the services staff only used the facilities on certain days. When they didn't, the car was supposed to be kept closed, and well, what was a simple lock to a slinker?

The slinkers were already gathering when Eli's group arrived. There were half a dozen of them, men and women of all ages. There was little similarity in their dress, either; it was clear they had come to slinking from as many different places as all the regular Train riders.

"Lucca!" hissed a middle-aged woman with auburn hair twisted in elaborate braids around her head. "How dare you bring normies here?"

Lucca squared his shoulders, and when he spoke, Eli guessed it was with more confidence than he actually felt. "They're not normies, Majenta. They're some new Kids."

"Really?" Majenta's tone was scornful, as if she didn't believe him. "How can children be slinkers? They're too noisy. No stealth. No style."

"They've already proved they have plenty of style," Lucca promised.

A swarthy man with an enormous mustache grinned at them. "Shove off, Majenta. Nothing says Road Kids can't be real kids." He squatted down in front of Willin and stuck out his massive hand. "I'm Durros. How old are you, sonny?"

Willin did not shake the hand that was offered to him, but obligingly held up three fingers. "I'm this many."

"And I'm four," Rinatta announced, not waiting her turn. "You're very hairy to be a slinker, I think," she added.

The man gave a great guffaw. "Indeed I am. Luckily, it's the boots that make the slinker." He tapped his foot on the ground, and Eli noticed he was wearing boots like Lucca's. Rinatta looked unsure if he was joking or not. Eli wasn't sure, either, but she introduced them all.

"They're mixed up in a bit of trouble," Lucca explained. "It's got the crooks all snorting and farting up a storm."

"Yes, I overheard some of them talking last night." Another woman came forward, dressed entirely in black, like Lucca. She was the most beautiful woman Eli had ever seen. Her skin was pale, but her lips were painted red. The hair that fell to her waist was coppery-gold. She wore a black cap on her head with a black lace veil that covered her eyes and nose. Eli could not guess her age.

The other slinkers made room for her, almost respectfully. "One of the conductors was talking about how he chased the missing nanny across The Train, when she vanished. Apparently, it was the second time they'd failed to catch her."

She looked curiously at Eli and the children, then drew a piece of paper out of a pouch on her belt. Unfolding it, she passed it to Eli. "They were posting these. It sounded so interesting, I thought I'd bring one to the meeting."

It was a flyer, like the one about slinkers Eli had seen. This one had three silhouettes stamped on it—a young woman, a girl, and a boy.

"That must be us!" gasped Eli.

"I'm sure it is."

Lucca frowned. "What does it say?"

The red-haired slinker read out loud: "Associates of the Exiled Vashani House. Wanted for suspicious activities and acts against The Train."

Eli felt her mouth drop open in despair. "How can we stay hidden if the whole Train knows about us?"

Through the veil, Eli could see the woman raise an eyebrow. "It seems to me you're already doing pretty well. And you have made a useful ally." She glanced at Lucca, who put his hands in his pockets and looked noncommittal.

"Enough yammering. It's time to chow down," said Durros. "I've got crab apples and beans. What else is there?"

"We can talk while we eat." The woman smiled. "My name is Cerci."

An empty hamper turned on its side made a table. There was a wide selection: hard-boiled duck eggs, fried rice, a container of ripe berries. Eli handed over some of the food bars, which Durros cut into little squares for dessert.

Eli showed Cerci the papers Sela had hidden in the pouch. "I think these are important but I'm not sure how." She explained what she had learned about the Baroness' exile.

"Sela told me I had to keep hiding until we reached Dongor. Then the new leader of the Rassa House is supposed to meet us. I don't even know what he looks like, or how he'll know us."

"The Rassa House? That is even more interesting," remarked Cerci, looking over to where Willin and Rinatta were playing with Durros.

"I mean, why come back at all?" sighed Eli. "The children were happy in Ugara, even if it was the middle of nowhere. What better life could there be in Dongorland if she'd have to hide all the time?"

"No, I'm afraid your Baroness is too cunning for that," said Cerci. "Politics, dear. It all comes down to politics."

"I am so sick of hearing that. It's politics, it's business. What difference does it make if nothing makes sense?" Eli rubbed her eyes.

"It may make a big difference. An enterprise as all-encompassing as The Train is necessarily a matter of great importance and of great wealth." Cerci leaned closer and spoke in a low voice. "Next week, all the leaders of the major Houses will gather in Dongor. The Train will stop there overnight, delivering people who wish to attend."

That was news to Eli. "So the Baroness didn't want to be left out?"

"I wonder." Cerci pursed her lips. "They are meeting to choose the new leader for the Rassa House. I'm afraid their Director passed away over a month ago, unexpectedly. He left no immediate heir, and the selection of a new Director must be voted upon. I believe several cousins are all claiming a right to it."

"What?" Eli was shocked. "They haven't picked a new Director yet? Who will meet us at the station?"

"The Rassa family is the biggest and most powerful clan of magic users. Dongor marks the first station in parts of the world where magic runs strong, and they control a lot of property there. But if I remember the rumors, it was the Rassa House that the Vashanis tried to seize, only a few years ago. Perhaps your Baroness thought the Director's death would be an ideal time to beg forgiveness?"

Eli could not imagine the Baroness begging forgiveness from anyone. She said so.

"Even if not, the conductors will surely hand the Baroness over to the Rassa House as soon as they arrive. That cannot be helpful to her plans, whatever they are. I doubt she will be welcomed after breaking Exile."

Eli frowned. "What about these papers, then? Birth certificates? Willin was born in Ugara. Will that make him exempt from any punishments? Oh, and there was also these." She reached in the bag and took out the little green bottles.

"What are they?" asked Cerci.

"I was hoping you knew," said Eli. "I don't know if I'm supposed to do something with them or not."

"Those are for blood magic." Majenta had come over from the other side of the car.

"Gross." Eli made a face.

"At least they're empty," Lucca remarked. "What do the labels say?"

Majenta took a closer look. "Blood of the woman. Blood of the man," she read, touching each bottle in turn. "Blood magic is very, very strong. Nothing breaks the ties of blood."

Eli nodded. She remembered Pria had told her the other Houses would blame Rinatta and Willin just for being the Baroness' kinfolk.

"What a messed up world," she muttered.

"It makes slinking look better," said Lucca. "You don't have to bother with other people's messes. You're free, really free, just to ride and go anywhere."

Eli took issue with that, too. "You aren't free. You make your own rules, but you still have to spend all this time getting around the rules for the rest of us."

Lucca shrugged. "Feels better, anyway. Slinkers keep to themselves, but they also look out for each other. Take something, leave something for the next person to come along. Use what you need, share what you can."

Cerci smiled at him. "Talk like that Lucca, it just reminds us of the first Road Kid we met. This one had the wanderlust in him from birth, I expect. It just took a few years to catch The Train."

Eli grinned, and Lucca looked sheepish.

"Hey, Cerci!" Durros shouted from across the room. He was standing, arms curled like thick branches, a child dangling from each bicep. "These kids are something else. Let's keep 'em." Rinatta and Willin shrieked in delight.

"It appears you've added another ally," Cerci observed. "Two, in fact," she added, quietly counting herself in.

Majenta rolled her eyes. "Well, that's it for all of us then. No one will cross Cerci."

Cerci grinned, her teeth fierce and white below her black veil. "I thank you for it, old friend," she replied.

The rest of the meeting, as far as Eli could tell, was simply for the slinkers to relax and enjoy each other's company. Eli enjoyed herself, too. They were strange comrades, but honest and devoted to their ways. The love they felt for The Train, Eli realized, was no less than that of folks like Pria and Uma, who spent entire lives saving for this rite of passage. They simply saw things differently, lived things differently. For slinkers, to ride was a right for all.

In the blue air of evening, they faded away, back to their own hideaways and sleeping spots. And then it was Eli's turn. She and the children vanished into the shadows of The Train.

She could never entirely remember the next few days. They were a blur to her, like the scenery flashing by outside The Train's windows, too swift to hold on to for more than a few seconds. She never slept longer than a few hours at a time, which no doubt accounted for much of the problem. When she thought about it, strange things stood out to her. An empty boxcar, dim and cavernous as a tomb, light filtering in through the slits of the ceiling. The smell of grease, on the night when she slept in the unoccupied cooks' car. Willin, giggling hysterically, as he peed off the side of a moving freight car. Or Lucca, cheerfully setting a match to a crumpled collection of slinker warnings and Wanted signs.

It was night when Eli felt The Train change again. A dreamy, wonderful feeling, rich and terrible all at the same time. The Train screeched and shuddered at the pull of new magic. The lanterns shivered from their usual amber glow and changed into flecks of blue-white light that drifted and moved across the ceiling with nothing to tether them. They glimmered along, like lost fish scales. To look at one, it did not seem to give off much light, but somehow, all together, their shine lit the car well enough.

"Will-o'-the-wisps," Lucca told her. "We'll reach Dongor tomorrow." He gave her hand a comforting squeeze.

Hope blew through her, and she knew they would make it. They had to.

But by morning, she was not so sure. There was an uneasy feeling on The Train, and the conductors were making rounds, examining tickets. Lucca slipped off to check in with the other slinkers. He did not return with good news.

"Durros says they got a tip on you. They know this is where you're planning to get off, since it's where they'll be handing over your Baroness. The conductors will be at every carriage door, monitoring who gets on and off. They're telling the passengers it's extra security because of The Train Houses gathering together, but Durros was convinced it's a set-up. They're going to nab you guys."

Eli wanted to stamp her foot, like Rinatta in the middle of a tantrum. "I've had enough of those conductors. How did they figure that out? Did they squeeze it out of Sela? They'd better not have hurt her."

"Durros says they're in an even bigger frenzy because you haven't turned up. They thought the kids would make it easy. You're making them look bad," Lucca replied.

"How are we going to get off? Go back through the roof, to the blindman's nest?" Eli said.

Lucca shook his head. "Coming down that ladder would be too risky for you guys. Dongor station is always packed and we'd be easy to spot."

"Well, there must be ways of getting out besides doors," said Eli.

"Oh, sure, there's plenty, but it's hard to say what's visible from the station sometimes." Lucca rubbed his eyes.

"How about we climb out the windows?" said Rinatta. Eli and Lucca stared at her, unaware she had been listening.

"Don't be silly," Eli chided her. "We'd look so ridiculous, everyone would come have a look."

Rinatta pouted.

"She may have an idea there," Lucca said slowly. "Only half The Train faces the platform. The other half goes down on the side of the tracks. It's not the easiest way to get back *on* The Train, but if you're looking to get off—The Train cars would completely obscure the view for anyone looking out from the station."

"What if it's a station with a raised platform?" protested Eli. "What are we supposed to do, tie bedsheets from the sleeper car into a rope? That only works in stories, Rinatta."

Lucca chuckled. "Wouldn't that make the old crooks lose their lunch when they came back aboard and figured out how we got away? But, no, I've been through Dongor enough times to tell you, the station is on flat ground. You kids can meet up with your mysterious Director and I'll have plenty of chances over the next day to slip back on board."

"But where can we get through unseen? Which windows aren't near the carriage doors?" Eli wondered out loud.

Lucca reviewed his knowledge of Train windows. "The third-class ones are the easiest to open, but there's sure to be conductors around. Second and first-class have air systems that help keep their cars cool or warm, so I rarely see windows open there. But I know they *can* open, in case the air system breaks down."

"I wonder..." She hesitated. "I wonder if they'd still be checking first-class compartments. Our old compartment was in a car that didn't have a main door."

Lucca's eyes lit. "That's it. Though it's hard to say which ones will be empty. It won't be sleeping time, so some of the passengers might stay in their seats."

It was Eli's turn to grin. "We don't need an empty car. Just one with people who won't turn us in right away."

As soon as The Train's wheels began to squeal and slow, they were on the move, making their way toward first-class one last time. They split up, hoping not to attract the attention of conductors keeping their eyes peeled for a young woman with two little ones. Eli and Willin went first, and Lucca and Rinatta followed more slowly.

The Train pulled into the station. Eli could hear voices shouting, "Dongor. This stop is Dongor. The Train rests here overnight." She rapped softly on the door to compartment fifteen. It seemed like years since she had been here last.

Nassan opened the door, his mouth falling in surprise when he saw her. Without a word, he beckoned her in. Eli felt her heart leap in gratitude.

"Eli! Willin!" Pria exclaimed when she saw them. She and Uma were in their regular spots. "Where's Rinatta?" the older woman added, her face growing worried.

"She's coming. She'll be here in a minute. We're so sorry to impose on you again. I promise, this is the last you'll see of us. You won't even have to lie if a conductor asks if you saw us."

"No apologies!" Nassan waved her words away. "You are friends. Am I correct?" He looked severely at the Ahns, who both, after a moment, nodded.

"It's good to see you," Pria admitted.

After a worrisome little while, Lucca and Rinatta joined them. Lucca surveyed the view from the window. The tracks were set in a narrow trench below them. "Perfect," he declared. "Now how do we open it?"

It proved tricky, for the window had been sealed a long time. With some force, Lucca managed to pry the clamps open and push the glass panel up.

"It's still a bit of a drop, if you're not used to that sort of thing. Perhaps those bedsheets would have been useful after all," Lucca joked. "I'll go first. Hopefully I can catch the rest of you as you fall."

His slinker feet climbed the wall of the car and he positioned himself on the window ledge. He leapt out, like a black bird taking flight.

"Rinatta, you're next. This was all your idea, remember," Eli told her.

"I'm not scared," proclaimed the girl. They hoisted her out the window and then dangled her as far down as they could. Lucca grabbed her legs and lowered her onto the gravel beside him. They bundled Willin out the same way.

"You have come all this way, protecting these children. I take pride in having known you. I am glad to have seen you one more time," Nassan told her with genuine feeling.

"Thank you," was all Eli could say. She felt moved almost to tears.

"Good luck," chirped Pria. "Oh Eli, be careful."

"I will. It's almost over."

Nassan offered her his hand, and she went out the window. She dropped awkwardly to the ground. The Train cast a deep shadow across them. There was no one else around.

"Keep close to The Train," advised Lucca. "We don't want anyone to look out the window and see us. We can't get cornered down here. Most stations like this have steps to get up to the rest of the station. We can slink onto the platform while they still think we stayed on board."

They hurried along, down past the passenger cars, toward the engine.

The Train snorted and snuffed, belching out a huge blast of air. Was it about to leave again, Eli thought in confusion?

"Dragons!" yelped Willin in terror.

Just beyond the first passenger car were harnessed two great dragons. Their hides were tough and scaled, like Nassan's lizard, only a hundred, a thousand, times larger. Their long jaws were crowded with teeth. They rolled their great bronze eyes almost to the back of their heads to look at the tiny humans. One coughed deep in its throat, and then both looked away, almost bored.

"Let's, uh, let's try the other way," Lucca stammered. "I should have remembered, it's not just will-o'-the-wisps that come after Dongorland. Magic runs all parts of The Train now."

"Do they eat people?" Willin asked as they hurried along.

"I don't want to find out," replied Lucca, most sincerely.

They went down the entire length of The Train. Boxcars, freight cars, cook cars. At last, the caboose, and just beyond it—yes! The stairs!

The rat-faced conductor stepped out from behind a car. Everyone froze.

His mouth was pulled in a grim line. His eyes were black and empty. He carried a short club. "All of you are under arrest," he said. "Surrender now and maybe no one will get hurt."

Eli felt a chill run through her. She didn't want to think about what that club could do to a little boy like Willin. Lucca seemed to have similar thoughts, as he slowly pushed the toddler to stand behind him. Eli was impressed; he didn't even try to weasel away.

"We're, we're not on The Train anymore," Eli said, desperately. "What authority do you have over us here?"

"The station belongs to the Railroad just as much," the conductor answered. "I answer to the Railroad. I answer to its laws."

Eli snorted. Somehow, things seemed ridiculous all of a sudden. To have come so far, only to be caught at the last second! What difference had it made?

"I might not have traveled as long or as far as other passengers, but I lived next to the Railroad all my life. The only law is to go on. Sure, there are some folks who think that money or family names make the laws, but those could change a thousand times and the Road will still be here. Still going on. Waiting for the next Train to pass and tear off the moss that covered the tracks since the last one came along. The moss will just grow back and the Road will just go on."

She stopped for breath. The conductor was looking at her curiously, as if he had never been spoken to like this before. Well, fine! Eli was downright annoyed by now. She was achy, and frightened, and tired beyond belief. Fine. If that meant coming along to jail, she might as well go, as long as she could get a full night's sleep there! At least this mess would be over.

She suspected the conductor, in his own way, must feel the same. His skin had that unhealthy color and his eyes were rimmed with shadows. With his hunt victorious at last, he could return to his normal Train duties.

He looks like he could use a nap too, Eli thought, with some small sympathy.

Naptime. Sleep. Yes, yes, yes!

Some place quiet and restful. You can be at peace for a few hours. Imagining the soft space of sleep, Eli began to sing her mother's soothe-charm at the conductor.

His body tensed, instantly suspicious. "Stop singing," he ordered.

But Eli kept on.

"Stop singing," he repeated. "Now!" He raised his club to strike her, but then his arm fell limp at his side. His fingers uncurled and the stick clanged to the floor. He gave a yawning cry of outrage, but his body crumpled, stricken by the blast of her spell.

"You killed him!" Lucca was appalled.

"Don't be silly!" Eli said. "He's only asleep. I always wondered how that charm would work in a place with real magic."

"You can do magic! I didn't know you could do magic!"

"Well, this was really my first try at anything, you know, important. I had no idea if it would work," she admitted.

"Apparently, you should always trust your crazy ideas," Lucca told her in deep appreciation.

"Come on! We have to get to the platform to meet up with this new Director. If he doesn't see us, maybe he'll leave." Eli wanted to get them back on track.

"Wait!" said Lucca. "I hope he won't mind if I borrow this…" After a bit of struggling, he peeled the conductor's jacket off and took the cap from his head. "Sometimes, it can be just as useful to hide in plain sight," he observed.

They made it up the stairs unhindered. As Lucca had predicted, the station was crowded. Eli wondered how many people had just gotten off of The Train for the night, and how many were city-folk, come to look at The Train. They scooted along through the teams of people, not sure who or what to look for next.

It was hard not be overwhelmed. Eli felt as if everything magical she had ever imagined was happening all at the same time. The skies above the city were filled with flying beasts, some with riders. A great white castle rose like a snaggley tooth out of the hillside.

They circled around and waited. And waited.

No one came.

"Let's go, Eli," moaned Willin.

But go where? She couldn't get back on The Train, like Lucca. It was too much to go on hiding and fearing all the time. She overheard two men gossiping in Traintalk about how many Railroad Barons were coming into town to witness the voting tomorrow. It was clear that the new Rassa Director had not yet been selected. Sela had been wrong. They had no friends in Dongor.

Indeed, it seemed as if enemies were filing in instead. A pack of guards marched up through the station, dressed in gray cloaks and carrying spears. They assembled in front of one of the cars.

A few moments later, several conductors escorted the Baroness and Sela out of The Train. They were both still wearing the same clothes they'd had on five days ago. The Baroness stood, tall and austere, but Sela looked shabby and old. How could they treat an old serving woman with so little respect?

The guard addressed the Baroness in a loud voice. "We are the officers of the Rassa Household. You are both charged with treason against The Train barons and for breaking your sentence of Exile. You must stand trial, but I assure you, it is only a formality. The punishment for returning from Exile is death."

Eli swallowed hard, glancing down at Willin and Rinatta. They were watching, but from their lack of reaction, Eli determined that they were not listening as attentively.

Why couldn't the new Director show up and reverse all of these horrible charges? Why would the Baroness go through all this trouble, if she knew she would be killed? And why even bother bringing along her children?

The children. They were somehow a key to this. The Baroness was not the type of woman who would have thought twice about leaving her family in Ugara while she conducted important business on her own. Why race with them back to

Dongor, to cast a vote on the Rassa House's heir? She was an Exile. There was no way for her to have any influence.

Or was there?

Was there something that would convince the Baroness she did have the power? Did she have something that would convince others?

Eli's thoughts turned slowly back to the papers from the bottom of Sela's emergency pouch. Birth records. Blood magic. Business wars and business marriages. Blood of the woman. Blood of the man. *Nothing breaks the ties of blood*, Majenta had said. Were there spells that proved such things? Did the Baroness think she had a claim to the Rassa House through blood? Through her children's blood?

Eli hardly dared think such things. And yet, she had never known anything but the villagers' rumors about the Baroness' husband.

Things crashed together in her mind, making her dizzy. But she had to do something, before it was too late. The guards were starting to march Sela and the Baroness off down the station.

"Rinatta!" yelled Eli. "Tell them to stop!" Rinatta stared at her, to see if she meant it. "Go! Go!" Eli insisted. "You can make them stop. Order them to stop."

"Are you crazy?" Lucca tried to fling out his arm to keep her next to him, but Rinatta pelted down after the guards. Eli, Lucca, and Willin all ran after her.

"Stop!" Rinatta shrieked, at ear-splitting volume. "Give me back my mommy!"

This last exclamation worked beautifully. The guards halted and stared at the tiny child, her hair flying crazily around her.

"You can't have my mommy," repeated Rinatta. "You hafta stop!"

The guard in front blocked Rinatta's path with his spearshaft. "Little girl, get out of the way." But another one called out, "She's the traitor's daughter. Might as well take her up to the castle, too. Shit, looks like the boy's here with her. It'll be a whole gallows family."

"You better not do that," Eli yelled. "This girl is your new director."

"What?"

The question came from several voices at once, from the guards and also from Lucca. Even Rinatta sneaked a look at Eli, unsure of what was going on.

"How do you figure that?" hissed Lucca. "Are you sure?"

"Yes," lied Eli. "I'm sure. It's the only thing that makes sense, anyhow."

"Is this true?" The guard in front seemed to be in charge. He turned toward the Baroness, still suspicious, but with a new wariness.

The Baroness and Sela regarded Eli with the same surprise. At last the Baroness spoke: "Yes. It is true."

"If you are lying—" the guard began.

"Blood cannot lie. Perform the spells," challenged the Baroness.

"That is not for me to decide," choked out the guard, looking more mystified than ever.

"Then bring us before those who can. It is a simple enough matter to sort out."

"Yes—er, yes, ma'am." The guard seemed to be rethinking his position, very carefully. "You all had better come along with us."

Eli let herself be taken prisoner. But the guards took great care in escorting them, careful not to jostle them or scare the children. *Let's hope this was the right thing to do.*

Perhaps even worse than the fear of hiding was the fear of waiting. To be sure, the Rassa clan received them more like honored guests than captured criminals, offering them wine and apricots soaked in honey. And yet, as Lucca pointed out, the walls of the castle courtyard were too high to climb.

"How much longer can this take?" she groaned. A sundial in the garden showed that over an hour had passed since the

Rassa spell-casters left with the Baroness' family and Sela to perform the ritual. It was the first time in weeks Eli had been away from Willin and Rinatta, and she found herself wild with unease.

"They said it wouldn't take long," Lucca reminded her. "Quit pacing."

"Sorry for dragging you along this far," said Eli, sitting down next to him in the grass. "I didn't want to take you away from The Train. I should have thought—"

"There's still half a day until The Train leaves again. I'm not off yet," he told her.

The gate to the courtyard swung open. A servant came in, giving them both a formal bow. He spoke in Traintalk, slowly, as if he wasn't used to it: "May I present the newly appointed Regent-Director of the Rassa House."

Eli and Lucca sprang to their feet. But it wasn't Rinatta who entered. It wasn't even the Baroness.

It was Sela.

"Sela? What's going on? Where are the children?" demanded Eli.

Sela wore a new tunic of jade green silk. "They are safe now. Matters have resolved themselves even better than I could have hoped. I thank you, Eli."

"But how? Why? Who *are* you?" Eli wondered if she had ever known.

"My name is Mehra Selanna Vasri Vashani. I served as the director for the Vashani House until our Exile three years ago."

"Vasri Vashani?" Eli echoed. "Are you the Baroness' *mother*?"

"Anya is my daughter, yes. When we came to Ugara, we wanted to keep a low profile, so I took the role of her servant. We planned to wait there until Rinatta was much older, but the Director of the Rassa House's untimely death forced us to move much earlier than we'd intended," Sela said.

"But I heard you got exiled because of the Rassa House. How can their Director be Rinatta and Willin's father?" Eli asked.

"The Vashanis and the Rassas had dealings with each other going back generations. Their father privately agreed to join with our House, but the rest of his clan found out before our proposition could be put into action. They couldn't take away his power as Director, so they charged us with an attempted takeover instead. They persuaded the other Barons that we alone had schemed to alter the balance of power on the Railroad. As Anya was with child at the time, Exile seemed the ideal stroke of justice. They never guessed they were sending away the heirs to their own fortune."

Eli shook her head in amazement over these peculiar business rulings. "So now instead of needing to vote on which relative will inherit the title of Director, Rinatta gets everything?" Her mind reeled at the thought.

Sela's smile was professionally modest. "Rinatta's first act as Director was to nullify the Rassas' charge of treason against the Vashanis. We are no longer breaking Exile." The smile deepened. "Her second act was to appoint me, her grandmother, as Regent-Director until she comes of age."

"Thank goodness!" Eli sighed in relief.

"She is only four," agreed Sela. "She has many years left until she assumes her role. In the meantime, she needs to be surrounded by people who know her, who care about her, and care what kind of woman she will become." Sela paused. "Eli, the service you have done our family can never be repaid. Without your cleverness and kindness, the children would never have been safe. If the Rassa clan had learned of them before we reached Dongor, I am certain they would not have stayed alive long enough for anyone to listen to their claim."

Eli was sure the rat-faced conductor wouldn't have hesitated to carry out such an order.

Sela turned to Lucca, who had been listening in fascination. "Young man, I do not know how Eli persuaded you to help her, but we are also in your debt."

Lucca shuffled his feet. "It was nothing," he said. "They were cool kids."

Sela took an envelope out of her pocket. "I have here two first-class tickets to ride The Train. Eli, you have come so far, but there is still so much of the world left to see. You can keep journeying, until you get to Sao Lindros and return home to your family. Or you can keep riding as far as The Train takes you. When you are not fleeing great peril, it is a wonderful place." She lowered her voice. "Or, if you choose, you are welcome to stay here in Dongor for a time. You can continue to work with the children, as their caregiver." Her tone made it clear she knew it was a strange request: years' more work, compared to a life of high adventure.

Eli didn't know what to say. She had already seen that The Train was a wonderful place. How exciting would it be to keep riding? To feel again the melody of the wheels on the track beneath her, every moment rushing toward something new? If she reached out her hand, she could take it.

From down the hall, she heard Willin laughing—he had the most absurd cackle. How good to hear it again! She felt a strange pang. She couldn't wait to see their faces. After all they'd been through, it would be so hard to say good-bye…

She didn't want to say good-bye. She wanted to see them. To stay with them, cuddle them, to play and laugh, and not be looking over her shoulder in fear every ten seconds.

Rinatta burst into the courtyard, braids streaming behind her. "Willin hitted me!"

"Tattle-tale," he accused.

"Oh, stop it, you two!" hollered Eli. She flung her arms around them and they bowled her over in a giant hug.

"Children, say good-bye to Eli now. She's getting ready to go back to The Train," Sela told them.

"You're leaving us?" Rinatta said.

"Um, no. I'm not going anywhere yet," Eli answered, and was almost deafened by screeching cheers.

"Yay!"

Willin and Rinatta each grabbed one of her legs, as if trying to stop her from ever getting away. Eli tried to shake them off but was laughing too hard.

"But we do have to go down to the station to see Lucca off, right?" She turned to him and smiled.

"Yeah, I think that's right." He smiled back.

"Awww," groaned Willin, and tried to attach himself to Lucca's leg now.

"We'll keep an eye on The Train schedule. We'll visit the station the next time it passes through. Will you come out and say hello?" said Eli.

"'Course!" promised Lucca. "If you ever get tired of these ragamuffins, you can always jump aboard with me."

"And if *you* ever get tired of slinking, you can drop by for a real visit with us! This castle is going to be our new home! It's huge!" Rinatta shouted.

Lucca raised his eyebrows. "Sounds like a plan," he said.

"So will we be needing these?" Sela asked, holding up one of the new tickets.

"Not for me," said Lucca. "I ride on my own."

"Not today," Eli amended for herself. "But let's save them, Sela. Someday, we'll need to ride again."

Her journey wasn't over, not forever. But for now, she had arrived.

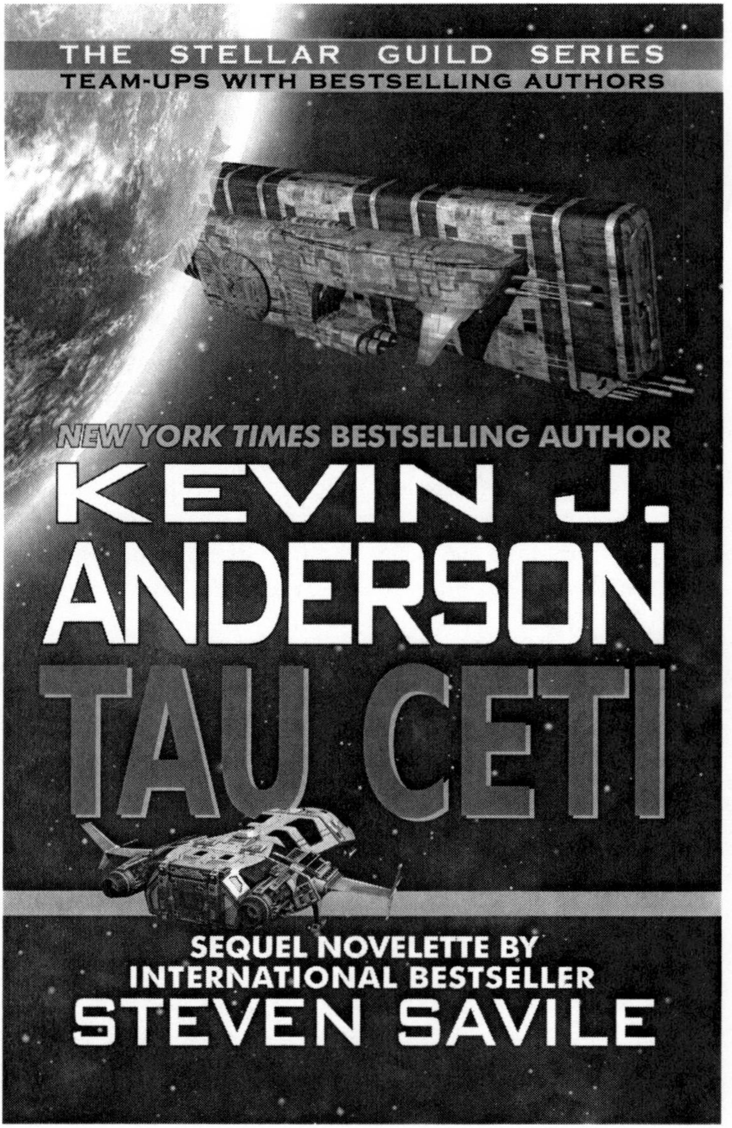
THE STELLAR GUILD SERIES
TEAM-UPS WITH BESTSELLING AUTHORS
NEW YORK TIMES BESTSELLING AUTHOR
KEVIN J. ANDERSON
TAU CETI
SEQUEL NOVELETTE BY
INTERNATIONAL BESTSELLER
STEVEN SAVILE

NEW YORK TIMES BESTSELLING AUTHOR

MERCEDES LACKEY
REBOOTS

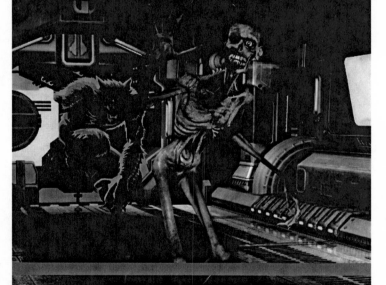

PREQUEL NOVELETTE BY
CODY MARTIN

CPSIA information can be obtained at www.ICGtesting.com
Printed in the USA
LVOW111325101012

302247LV00001B/19/P